Jealous Enough to Murder

Fourth in the Grand Auntie Mystery Series

J.E. Armstrong

O beware, my lord, of jealousy!
It is the green-ey'd monster which doth mock
The meat it feed on. --William Shakespeare,
The Tragedy of Othello, Act III, Scene ii

Printed in the USA

ISBN: 979-8-9878304-3-7

Dedication

To old friends and new ones. Both are precious—even the ones who never meant all they said.

Acknowledgements

"This solitary work we cannot do alone," a freshman wrote to me in COMP 101 years ago. That level of realization from so young a writer struck me then and strikes me now as a profundity beyond her years. (For the curious—I'm sure I rewarded her with an *A*!).

The fact remains: We do need others—others secure enough in themselves, in our friendship, and with the act of writing to comment on the good, bad, and ugly I offer. I am blessed to be surrounded by those who willingly and honestly supply me with appropriate feedback and support me with their encouragement. If I listed them all, the list would take more pages than this book allows.

So, by groups, I extend my thanks to:

All my true friends
All my special friends
The occasional *bon ami*
My Writing Group
My Book Club
My students—past and present
My fans
Former Abydos Trainers
Those who love mysteries
Those who love reading
Those who love writing
Those who love life

Mizjaq Green, my artistic colleague, who seems to intuit the exact design needed for the right cover and formatting of each of my books, deserves a singular shout-out. She is a spatial genius!

And, as always, I acknowledge and thank my husband, Eddie, artist, and writer himself, who contently sits back letting me dabble, experiment, tinker and fiddle with words and characters, plots and twists, beginnings and endings with the utmost patience and forbearance, treating the results with nothing but superlatives. How did I get so lucky? **The process is with us all!**

Praise for *JEALOUS ENOUGH TO MURDER*

In her fourth novel, the Grand Auntie of Sleuthdom prepares to attend a wedding in Scotland that unites old friends and triggers bygone resentments.

A mysterious note written on expensive paper, missing minaudières, rich locations, and a mixed cast of characters come together to tell the story of sisters with unresolved feelings that fester over time resulting in murder.

Part mystery, part love story, and part cautionary tale about holding grudges, *Jealous Enough to Murder* explores how relationships evolve over time, the pomp and glamor of aristocracy, and how we use abductive reasoning to understand people's motivations and make sense of the most profound events. --Nicole E. Klimow, PhD

With the ease of a long-time friendship, joining Grand Auntie and her beau, Aladar Gallant in *Jealous Enough to Murder* the reader is wrapped up in adventure, word play, and tidbits of knowledge. Traveling from New Jersey, to Scotland, to the Poconos Mountains, the mystery and clues have you sitting on the edge of your seat and turning the pages.

J. E. Armstrong has carefully and meticulously crafted a series that refuses to allow you to put each book down. *Jealous Enough to Murder*, the fourth in the Grand Auntie Mystery Series, will not disappoint the reader. It has not disappointed me but rather allowed me to sit as with a friend and enjoy the story. --Dr. Maria Isabel Corona

My favorite in the series so far. But already I can't wait for the next one. These are each so unique. No cookie-cutter formula for Armstrong! --Joel Brennon

**Chapter One**

Ever since my older sister Gladys announced her intention to marry Dr. Samuel Henson, the family has been in the throes of preparation. As usual, I write to my deceased husband Duarte, to help me bring order out of such chaos. The writing helps me re-think things, place them in perspective, and often yields insights. Somehow, writing focuses my thinking and then reading what I have written yields levels of meaning for me.

Now everyone is at breakfast, so I'm stealing a few minutes to write Du.

My Beloved Du,

As you can imagine the family is in a state of happy shock over Grammy Gladys' intention to marry Dr. Henson. (I guess we'll always call him doctor.) He has been her doctor for over fifty years—maybe more. No one knows her better.

You probably wonder what took him so long to propose. Apparently, being old school, he felt unworthy in the sense of wealth. Even though he is what we would call 'a man of means,' given Gladys' immense fortune, he believed his money no match for hers.

But fate stepped in. Some shirt tail uncle in Scotland remembered him or his mother or them both and bequeathed our Dr. Henson a sizable fortune, the title of Viscount, and an historic castle, Inverlochy, in Scotland.

Yes, Du, an actual castle. Then, and only then, did Dr. Henson propose. Gladys accepted and why not? She has everything but a title. Besides, I think she has long loved him.

And as you can further imagine, knowing Gladys, she has taken the reins of the planning, orchestrating us as if we were a business, not a family. She is nothing if not efficient.

That trait helps explain her tremendous successes with her world-wide floral business and now with PARA: The Portal to Advancing Research on Aging, which she affectionally refers to as "my Shangri La." Both enterprises have made her the multi-millionaire she is today (some say billionaire—that's with a b).

Ever style conscious, even at ninety-three (although with this new ointment of hers—JUNGYU— she really does look in her seventies), she contacted "The House of Chanel." She actually called them at 31 Rue Cambon, Paris, France.

They were delighted to provide her with everything she could possibly need for a flawless event—for a hefty fee, of course—but that's to be expected, and she can afford it, Lord knows. Needless to say, with Chanel in charge, Glady, her bridal party, and the family will be attired in only the most superlatives of Haute Couture.

Since money is not an issue, I believe Glady intends to fly us over to Paris for our fittings, although we may leave from Scotland not New York. I can't wait. Ever since you and I visited that magical City on the Seine, it has been my favorite. Know I will be thinking of you constantly while there.

Glady's house and mine here in Bricksbourgh, connected as they are by next-door proximity, have been turned into beehives of activity. First, Chanel is already sending us samples of fabrics and colors, mostly shades of white—so our doorbells ring throughout the day, a constant reminder of wedding bells. Soon, if I understand the arrangement correctly, they will send their couturiers directly here for the first fittings. After that, the fittings will take place in Paris!

Second, every florist who ever worked in any way with Glady has sent flowers, bouquets, and rare blooms of congratulations; and, probably and more importantly to them, for the purpose of giving Glady ideas and garnering her favor. Florists everywhere are vying for contracts for this wedding. They know Gladys, so they know it will be a news-worthy event without bounds.

"What are we to do with all of these?" I asked her as I casually picked up one especially unusual bloom.

"Be careful, Lisbet, that's a juniper-leaf grevillea and it's sometimes prickly."

I immediately dropped the spider-like flower.

"That's one symbolic flower," I say, "pretty but dangerous, hardly appropriate for a wedding."

"Lisbet, you always look into everything so deeply," Glady commented, "you find layers of meaning in everything. You love symbolism."

I suppose I do. Is that a bad thing, Du? I always thought that made me interesting. But I didn't engage Glady in philosophical thought at that moment. I simply returned to my dilemma, by repeating my question, "We have flowers everywhere. What shall we do with them?"

"Enjoy them," she said.

Easy enough, I thought, but I turned away from the prickly spider flowers to recognizable docile daisies.

Third, Du, we have all the PARA communications bombarding us. Glady was smart to put Ande's husband Boris in charge of PARA. Boris chose now to launch the notifications about that magical ointment, JUNGYU, which Ande followed up with press releases and teasers. Since then, the inquiries and pre-orders have literally flowed in. Apparently, the world wants to look and feel younger—almost instantly—and that singular quality is one of the promises of JUNGYU. And, of course, Glady is her own best advertisement.

Loraine and Sea are doing a fine job keeping up. I think inviting them to serve on TEAM PARA has been therapeutic (and a wise decision by Glady). PARA appears especially good for Sea, who has been vacillating among the five stages of Kubler-Ross' theory

[4]

of grief since Trés' murder. Now, I think he finally may be in the 'acceptance' stage. Perhaps because of the new puppy, and perhaps because of their role in PARA as Operations Management Directors, Sea and Loraine don't have much time to brood.

Russ, the numbers genius of the family that he is, maintains the finances in good order, and his wife Pheme continues to amaze us all with her loving control of their newly born twins. Du, those two cupcakes are my joy!

Anne Henriette seems to be the aggressive one whereas Louise Elizabeth is more like me—reflective.

Ande, just a while ago, bought them a karaoke machine, which they love—who knew? And not long after that Pheme announced she is expecting again! As Lewis Carroll wrote in the Jabberwocky, *'O frabjous day! Callooh! Callay!'*

Doctor Ali told Pheme she is in excellent health and will have no problem traveling or delivering for that matter. She told her, "As a matter of fact, Young Lady, all the walking you'll be doing in Scotland will be good for you. I suspect you'll sleep soundly even on the plane, especially on the return flight."

I think I've already told you the wedding will be in Scotland—actually in the castle Dr. Henson inherited or on the castle grounds or both—depending upon the weather. (More on that in my next missive.) But sufficive to say at this point that Glady has hired a private plane

[5]

and two pilots to take all the family—Gladys, Dr. Henson, Ande, Boris, Sea, Loraine, Pheme, Russ, their twins, Joyce Elizabeth, Aladar, and me—as well as the key help—Jadwiga, Wald, Bridget, and Perla—to and from Scotland—and to and from Paris. The plane seats twenty, plus we are taking Coco, of course. (You know how they love dogs in Paris. Remember when we ate in that swanky restaurant next to a table with a poodle seated as if a guest? Remember how we gawked? That poodle was so well-bred, it only put its paws, not its elbows on the table! Of course, we won't be introducing Coco to any restaurants, but I don't think the French will mind her a bit—or the Scottish either for that matter.)

I thought we'd be taking Sea's puppy, Sapphire, to Scotland, too, but maybe not. At this point, Sea and Loraine are deciding whether to leave her with friends or not. Much as I love dogs, leaving her would probably be the best since she's a good seventy pounds.

The final piece of news is our dear Pheme has lighted on the idea of sharing a ghost story during our stay in Scotland. Since we will be there for a month or so, Pheme thinks one night given to a spooky story would be 'fun.' The idea germinated after she ran across a story with Dr. Henson's castle's name in its title, "The Ghosts of Old Inverlochy Castle." I suppose since ghosts are a staple in Scottish lore, everyone will love a ghost story. Still, at my request, she's to read it to Aldar and me and the family one evening in the next day or so.

[6]

Then we can judge its appropriateness. I never heard of a ghost story before a wedding, have you? I'm hesitant. I don't want it to dampen the joy of the event. Aladar thinks it's a great idea! What do you think, Du?

Until next time...

Chapter Two

We gathered in the library of my home. Perla had prepared refreshments for us—several charcuterie boards complete with a variety of cooked and smoked meats surrounded by foreign and domestic cheeses, kosher dill pickles, stuffed and unstuffed olives and mushrooms, raw but edible veggies such as radishes, sliced avocados, green onions, carrots, celery, patio tomatoes, cucumber slices and chunks of jicama. She added an array of breads, baguettes, crackers, and accompanied it all with complimentary spreads, garnishes, sauces, dips and marinades. There were condiments for every palate. We could have invited an army. And, of course, there were plenty of libations, too.

"Hi everybody!" Pheme began.

Even though Pheme is in her late thirties and has twins, she has that schoolgirl quality about her. She greets the world with an innocence and freshness that always makes me smile.

"When Grammy Gladys told us she was marrying Dr. Henson who had inherited a castle in Scotland, I did some research. The twins love to go to the library, pull out the books on the bottom most shelf in the baby book section, and look at the pictures. So, I took them and settled them in. That gave me time to explore 'Old Inverlochy Castle.'"

"Were you looking for Scottish history?" Aladar asked.

"Actually, yes. I don't know much about Scotland except what we studied in school—*Macbeth* and all. I didn't want to go over there embarrassing our family by looking or sounding like a dunderhead."

I laughed. Pheme could pull out some unusual words sometimes. "No one would think you a dunderhead, Pheme," I assured her, "Please share the story you unearthed."

"I found lots of history and a specific story about the place—Inverlochy. People named Comyns first built a wooden structure on the property way back in the 1200s as a sign of power. Then Oliver Cromwell rebuilt it as a fort on the same land in 1690. Dr. Henson's ancestors replaced the wooden fort with stone, so it became something closer to a castle than a fortress."

"Fascinating," said Aladar, who always supports Pheme no matter how zany her ideas or far out her statements.

"But what really caught my eye was a ghost story that takes place in that castle—in the actual castle where we will be staying and where Grammy will be married. Grand Auntie wants me to read it to you so the family can all decide if it's appropriate to share with all the guests during one of our evenings in Scotland."

[9]

"Read it, Pheme," Aladar urged as if he were following a script.

"To be totally honest, I did doctor it up a bit. See what you think."

I chimed in. "Come on, Pheme, read it!"

At this point in the evening, we all were curious as well as satiated with food and drink, all readied and relaxed to hear a good story. We began to chant, "Read it."

"Okay. Here goes," said Pheme unceremoniously. She commenced by shaking the papers in her hand and making her voice sound deeper and spooky. We tried not to laugh; she was so serious about it.

The Ghosts of Inverlochy Castle

Once upon a time in a place called the 'Land of the Scots,' there lived a wealthy merchant named Balloc, whose name means 'bull' for he was strong of body and strong of heart but jealous by nature. This Balloc and his wife Abria, which means 'gentle,' had a beautiful daughter they named Tegan, their 'Little Storyteller.'

Pheme, as she read, made air quotation marks around the words "Bull," "Gentle," and "Little Storyteller."

"Pheme, do you need to give the meaning of each name? Doesn't that bog down the story?" I asked.

"Grand Auntie, that's what I added. I thought since this is a fairy tale, the names should be significant."

"I think the meaning of the names important to know," defended Aladar.

"Well then, please proceed." I was clearly outnumbered; and, after all, I reasoned to myself, this isn't a class, this is an event.

"I am going to build you a magnificent castle, Tegan," Balloc told his daughter one day as they sat in the garden enjoying the breeze from the sea.

"*Tapadh leat, Athair*," Thank you, Father, responded the sweet and gentle Tegan.

Hearing those ancient Celtic words from the lips of his daughter just made Balloc love her all the more.

And so, the castle was built under the watchful eyes of Balloc's architect. "Make the walls thick and strong," Balloc commanded. "And make many, many rooms after the fashion of the labyrinths of ancient Egypt. But within those rooms, create one of gold. Make it secure and hard to find, instructed Balloc. I have plans for that room. No one is meant to find it."

You see Balloc, being a jealous man, held tightly to his money, his land, his castle, and to his beautiful daughter. He never intended to share her with anyone else.

His architect, bowing respectfully, replied, "As ye wish, Sir." And so, work went on for many, many months.

[11]

When the castle was finally finished, Balloc issued a proclamation that went out far and wide throughout the kingdom and beyond:

Any suitor trying for the hand of the daughter of Balloc and Abria from the land of the Scots is welcome. But to win her hand, the suitor must find her in the golden room, a room hidden amongst the many rooms in Inverlochy Castle. He must conquer the challenge issued in that room, then and only then, claim her for his bride. Failure means death.

The story goes that Abria thought this harsh, but Balloc was adamant.

Suitor after suitor traveled to Inverlochy Castle. Many tried one or two rooms, only to resign themselves to failure and death. Some made it to five rooms only to abandon the task as hopeless. They died, too. A few conquered ten rooms but wandered forever afterward within the intricate castle labyrinth. None made it to the golden room and the beautiful Tegan.

Still they came. Still they tried. Still they failed.

"Don't you think you should describe the challenge in the golden room?" Ande asked.

"That might really bog down the story," Aladar argued, as usual taking Pheme's side.

"They typically don't go into that much detail in fairy tales. But that gives me an idea," said Pheme, "If we want, we can spend some time after the story

[12]

making up challenges for the golden room. That would be fun!" Pheme suggested.

Aladar added, "We could offer prizes, fun prizes!"

Everyone liked those ideas. I prodded, not wanting us to lose the thread of the story, "We could do both those things, but please keep reading, Pheme."

In time, Abria left forever for Ath-bheatha, and soon after that Balloc was called by the gods to join Abria in the Otherworld. This left Tegan all alone, all alone and lonely. Hour after hour she sat by herself, day after day, week after week, month after month the beautiful Tegan sat isolated and forlorn.

The townsfolk worried. They would watch the castle but only catch glimpses of Tegan between the arrowslits and crenellations as she walked her solitary walks. Soon they told stories of Tegan looking like a ghost as she had grown thin and wore only a white flimsy gown no matter how cold the weather. These stories, as is the way of oral tales, became more and more ghastly. Tegan became a ghost.

Finally, Keridwen, the Celtic shape-shifting goddess of inspiration who had been observing Tegan all this time, reached down into her cauldron of wisdom and created a son. She named him Taliesin. He was handsome of face and bright of mind.

When Tegan first saw Taliesin, she immediately fell in love with him. When Taliesin first saw Tegan, he immediately fell in love with her.

Keridwen then blessed them as she tied a golden twine around their wrists, "I unite you in love and happiness. May you live long, rule wisely, and be kind to your subjects." With that Tegan and Taliesin reigned for a thousand and one years in great love and happiness and with great prudence.

The people of Inverlochy to this day will tell you that they often see Tegan and Taliesin roaming the castle as they look after their subjects. On starry nights, when the moon is full, they claim they can hear Tegan telling her stories. When the breeze blows, the townsfolk will tell you how Tegan and Taliesin talk to each other, tease each other, laugh and giggle.

Thus, Keridwen began the Scottish custom of tying the hands that continues to this very day.

Here Pheme stopped her reading the story to say, "Grammy Gladys and Dr. Henson will continue honoring this custom at their wedding ceremony with what is now called 'handfasting.'" Then folding the pages of the story, she leaned back in her chair and concluded with: THE MORAL OF THE STORY: LOVE CONQUERS JEALOUSY"

Pheme stopped. When she looked up, she saw everyone staring at her.

"What?" she asked.

"Why, that's beautiful, Pheme," I said, "and it's totally appropriate for Grammy. May she find such love and happiness. As I hugged dear Pheme, Aladar added, "and with JUNGYU may she live a thousand and one years!" We laughed and toasted Grammy even in absentia. That single evening heralded the beginning of what was to be a typical Grammy Glady extravaganza.

**Chapter Three**

"My heavens!" I exclaimed upon opening my mail.

"What is it?" asked Perla.

"An invitation to my 65th University Graduation Reunion! Can you believe it's been sixty-five years?" I didn't wait for Perla's reply.

"Well, I can't believe it. Besides, I can't deal with this invitation right now anyway with all the goings-on for Glady. Perla, please put this invitation somewhere safe, mark the calendar, and remind me about it when I return from Scotland."

Just then the phone pinged. Picking it up without checking the caller I.D., I heard a voice from the past, "Hi, Elizabeth. This is Angelique Forester, Gregoria University Class of '59. Do you remember me?

Through the mist of time and memory, a sweet-faced girl emerged, one with auburn hair cropped close to her face and beautiful big green eyes that spoke volumes. She served as class president our senior year and proved to be a born leader. "Of course, I remember you, Angelique! What brings you to the phone after all these years?"

"I just received my invitation to our 65th Class Reunion. I assume you received yours, too. Can you believe it—sixty-five years?"

[16]

"No, I cannot, I really cannot. I just expressed that very sentiment to Perla as I opened my invitation."

"Perla?"

"Perla is my right hand, caregiver, housekeeper, girl Friday."

"How nice. Well, I hope you plan to attend the reunion," Angelique said.

"Presently I'm in the midst of my older sister's wedding plans, but once the wedding is over, I intend to give the reunion my time and effort. It's not until October, right?"

"No! Actually, it's the first weekend in November. Oh, but do attend. And as a kind of a pre-reunion, I'm inviting those of us who live in the New York City vicinity to High Tea at my place—you know, to get re-acquainted before we get re-acquainted. Please squirm out of any familial obligations and come."

"When and where?"

"Next Thursday. I live in the upper East Side of the City—easy to get to. Just take a cab. I'll text details. High Tea-time, about 5-ish. Do come."

Angelique, like most of the girls in my tiny class of twenty-seven, "comes from money"—old money. In Angelique's case, lots of money, lots of old money. On her mother's side, it's the Rockefeller's fortune; on her father's side, it's the Astor's wealth. Coming from the owners, at one time or another, of two of the most prestigious hotels in NYC, the Waldorf Astoria and the

[17]

Plaza, caused people to refer to Angelique's family as the "landlords of New York." This gives Angelique a patina, a finish that screams 'class.' Besides that, Angelique (and we never called her by any abbreviation) is a lovely, kind, giving person. I most definitely wanted to attend her high tea.

"425 Park Avenue," I told the cabbie.

"Yeah. OK Miss Goin' to somethin' fancy dancy?"

Of all the cab drivers in the City, I had to get a chatty cabby, I thought.

"What makes you ask that?"

"That address. That's the big one. The Big Cheese. The Big Apple, if youse get my drift."

Dear, God, save me from this jabberer. "Well, if you must know, I'm visiting a friend."

"Muss be a rich friend."

"You could say that."

"Ain't none of my business," *Right you are*! I thought but kept my tongue. "But tell youse friend to be extrey careful. There's been more 'activity,' if youse get my drift, up that way lately. Word on the street is the mob is prowlin for someone, revenge thing, makes it risky for everybody, if youse get my drift."

"I'll be sure to warn her."

"You be extrey careful, too. Older woman like youse with all those kinds of rings on, if youse get my drift. Thugs'll just rip 'em right off youse fingers. Rip youse fingers off, too. Be extrey careful. Turn them

[18]

stones around when youse are on the street. Just sayin'."

Now that's sweet of him. He may be gabby but he's well intentioned.

We rode a short time in blessed silence.

"Here youse go." He said as he pulled up in front of Angelique's high rise. I started to get out when he fairly shouted, "Wait! Wait! I'm gonna' hail the doorman."

With that my 'knight in a checker cab' motioned the doorman over. To him he said, "Hey youse, take care of this here lady." To me he said, "Don't want youse walkin' even that short ways by youseself outta *my* cab if you get my drift. I'd feel real bad if anythin' happened."

"Thank you. Thank you very much." I smiled as I gave him a generous tip—the doorman, too.

[19]

**Chapter Four**

Even though I live in a Brownstone on the Upper Eastside about half the year, I'm always impressed with those massive structures on Park Avenue also on the Upper East side. Just the lobbies are breathtaking with all that glass and steel and art. Angelique Forester's place, housed in one of those skyscrapers, was no exception.

With a doorbell that rivaled the Westminster chimes, her foyer immediately dazzled me as I entered it directly from her private elevator, where they apparently periodically sprayed a lovely but not overpowering perfume.

Her entry way with its twelve-foot beamed ceiling and huge soundproof windows allowed Southern exposure but forbad any City noise. I stepped into a soundproof room with only a hint of classic music playing somewhere. Inviting, too, were works of art and collector's prints that graced the large gallery that led from that foyer directly into her spacious living room.

I immediately spotted several of my former classmates already gathered in and around Angelique's impossibly large oval egg-shell white tufted sofa. Age and years of breeding prevented us from squealing in delight at the sight of each other, but low-keyed chuckling and deep smiles underlined our talk of the "good old days."

I hadn't seen Hanaka Haruki since graduation in 1959 and was eager to chat with her, especially since Grammy loved Japan so much. I mostly wanted to talk to her about that cherry tree in Grammy's front yard. Grammy cherished and guarded that tree like the tree hugger she was, but the tree was aging; I didn't want her to lose it. Maybe Hanaka knew some tricks that would extend its life. I often thought that tree personified Glady. I thought it harbored secrets.

"That's an alpine cherry tree," Gladys told me once, "it should outlive me." Zeroing in on Hanaka, I noticed she wore stylish dark glasses with designer frames. I wondered about those glasses, straining my mind to remember if Hanaka wore glasses back in the day—certainly not dark glasses and certainly not inside during the day. *The good nuns wouldn't have allowed it,* I thought.

But before I could make my way in Hanaka's direction, Cathy Melather, the class gossip, grabbed my arm and said in her cheeky way, "As I live and breathe, you look exactly like you did in college. Tell me your secret." I was about to tell her about JUNGYU when the ever-stately Umbuya Dumbuya glided in our direction, holding, as I always remember her holding, balancing really, a cup of tea—*steady as ever even at this age.* I thought.

As she drifted over, I replayed in my head the day we all met Umbuya. We were in Freshman

[21]

Composition 101. Professor Adrian asked each of us to introduce ourselves. One by one we gave predictable, rather mundane autobiographies—our name, we each claimed a mother, father, a sibling or two, a connection to Methodist or Catholic or some recognizable religion—no one claimed to be an atheist or agnostic. We all mentioned attending church camps, liking sports, playing tennis, golf, bridge—that kind of thing.

Then Umbuya stood up—towering, regal, over six feet we found out later, with ebon skin—and three beautifully mysterious tiny horizontal scars imprinted like perfectly formed crows' feet radiating from the external corner of each eye. Later in our friendship, I learned those marks were a permanent visual sign of status in her family.

She began, "I am Umbuya Dumbuya, the eldest daughter of the favorite wife of the present Chief of Sierra Leone. I have ten brothers and fifteen sisters. My mother is the Chief's favorite wife. I am a Christian."

We all gasped. There we sat all comfortable in our Western Caucasian-ness, but before us stood a princess, a real princess, yet a humble princess. As the year passed, we all grew to love and respect this woman. Watching her now just made me proud knowing she had established since graduation a non-profit organization to improve education in her country. Still beautiful, still regal, still able to balance that teacup. *Not bad for eighty-five,* I thought.

[22]

In close proximity to Umbuya, stood Frances Kearney, our beloved quiet Franny, always ready to help any one of us at any time, especially with math. As she sipped a Cosmopolitan, I thought, *where had I heard she had turned to tippling?* Franny rounded out the group—six of us.

"Before we take tea," Angelique announced, "allow me to show you around my home."

"Please do," encouraged outspoken Cathy, "we're all dying for a tour." *Same old Cathy,* I thought, *queen of straightforward hyperbole.*

As we all huddled behind Angelique like baby ducks, she led us first to the kitchen.

"I'm most proud of the kitchen area (not that I cook much)," Angelique added as an aside and a sideways smile, "but I did have a hand in designing it. Truth be told, Girls, I am in the custom manufacturing business. My goal is to make living easier for oldsters, those handicapped, or those who need some assistance. The social circuit got wearisome. While I loved the luncheons, teas, fund raisers, and galas, I needed to feel intrinsically productive, not extrinsically productive. All that folderol began to seem superficial. Although important to charities, I needed something more."

"I understand," I said. The others mumbled agreement. I asked myself *do they really agree?*

[23]

"What's the name of your business?" asked Franny.

"STREAM-A-LINE."

"I like it—short and to the point," I said.

"So then, let's begin there," suggested Angelique.

With that, the group of us stepped into what could best be described as a 'Chef's Kitchen.' Ohs and Ahs went around as we noticed the perfect LED lighting, the abundant counter space, and the unique cabinetry. Everything was designed to be eye level and within reach, which made this kitchen a dream for oldsters. We almost salivated when we spotted the pot filler faucet over the stove, "No carrying heavy pots, Girls!" Angelique told us.

Proudly but not in boast, she added, "I designed the shelves, so they are layered and moveable for convenience and easy viewing. They are also staggered in height in such a way so that nothing sits behind anything else."

I found myself wondering, *why aren't all homes aren't so equipped?*

"Look at these drawers," Cathy commanded, indiscreetly pulling out a few. "Drawers, lots of them, and some are deeper than others."

"Yes," Angelique agreed, not a bit bothered by Cathy's indiscretion nor worried about what we might see in those drawers. "I wanted them to swing out or around, making every bottle, box, bowl, container, can, dish, pot, or cooking utensil accessible. But what makes every person with some limitations swoon, are the pedals."

"Pedals?" we chorused. None of us had noticed any pedals.

"See?" With that Angelique stepped on one. We witnessed how all those shelves and drawers could easily be raised, lowered, moved, or swung around with a tap of the toe. *No back-breaking stooping,* I thought.

Hanaka kept running her hand along the elongated quartz breakfast bar as if to memorize it. She still wore those impossibly dark glasses. I continued to wonder about that.

Looking around, I noticed the top-of-the-line appliances. I recognized the oversized Wolf oven, the built-in microwave by Jean-Air, a Miele dishwasher, and a Sub-Zero top-bottom fridge/freezer—all the big names. Drool. Although none of us lacked anything, this was a dream kitchen. *Move over Julia Child! Welcome to the Techno-age!*

"Just off the kitchen, behold the additional eating area," Angelique continued her tour gracefully indicating the direction of an anteroom. "This area easily accommodates dinner parties of ten to twelve people." I noted the perfectly appointed table already set for our High Tea.

"Of course, we have a doorman full time, a community roof-deck pool, a splash pad for children, tennis courts, and event space with some stunning City views." Angelique said in that tone of voice that conveyed the sense—doesn't everyone? —without sounding condescending.

"I hate to be nosy, Angelique, but what about laundry?" I asked. What I didn't see was anything resembling a washer or dryer, iron or ironing board.

"Oh, that's the best part of all! Jane comes in twice a week to gather all the soils and refresh everything with spotlessly clean sterilized linens and towels and such. I don't even know when she arrives or leaves, she's so unobtrusive. And she even irons our sheets and pillowcases!" Angelique crowed. If I didn't know Angelique was innately humble, even though she was born with that proverbial 'silver spoon,' I'd have thought she was bragging.

Spacious bedrooms with high ceilings held generous closets and storage space with detailed millwork trim that added an elegant touch to each room. Custom blinds, both remote and hidden, controllable, and motorized—as were the lights—were available by a single clap of the hands or snap or crook of a finger.

A massive marble bath adjoined each bedroom, and each bathroom featured a large jacuzzi, a soaking tub, and a custom shower. Examining each shower, I

[26]

saw recessed body sprayers strategically placed overhead as well as along the sides of its walls. A comfortable, adjustable slatted wooden seat lined one side. My thoughts immediately shot to Aladar. *Why am I thinking of Aladar?* I asked myself. *Why not?* I answered.

"I'll wager you are all absolutely famished after the tour," Angelique ventured, interrupting what might have been the beginning of another one of my Aladar fantasies. We nodded like good little ducklings and traipsed behind her into the dining area.

"What a feast you have laid," commented Umbuya. We all murmured our agreement as we studied the tiered dishes of crustless sandwiches of all kinds and the platters of sliced roasted beef, chicken and lobster salad sandwiches on buttered brioche.

The colorful sushi rolls with salmon and capers accompanied the imported cream cheeses and bagels. Nut meats sat side-by-side candied goodies while fruits such as lucuma cherimoya, durian, kiwano, jackfruit, dragon, and carambola were beautifully arranged along with some exotic ones I didn't recognize.

There were trays of every chocolate imaginable. Additional trays of tempting delicate desserts were too close to me as were the appealing kind you shouldn't eat if you're watching your waistline.

I found piles of cookies, too, including my favorite—macaroons, *and* macarons in assorted colors.

[27]

Of course, here and there along the tables sat robust pots of exotic teas with choices of cream, milk, skim milk, or lemon wedges.

"Here's to the Duchess of Bedford, Anna Maria Russell, who, I understand, is responsible for introducing High Tea to America in the early 1800s, Angelique said, raising her teacup in toast, "I hope my chef has done her justice. Please everyone, find your places and make yourselves comfortable."

We all scurried to find our individual place cards. Angelique had them done in calligraphy.

"It's my pleasure to have you all here today as a prelude to our upcoming reunion." "Here! Here," we responded taking our seats.

Chapter Five

Angelique doesn't remember me at all, Jane realized after her first visit to Angelique's high rise and briefly passing by her. *Smart of me to apply for that position of laundress through Edjoy Realty instead of directly with Angelique. I can come and go and rarely see her or her me. But why would she remember me? She ignored me then, why would she recognize me now?*

But I remember her. With that thought, Jane entertained a personal reverie. *I wanted to be so good in grammar school to impress the nuns. I wanted them to love me. I tried to get their attention, too; I begged for it, "Sister Rose, let me water the plants." "Sister Sheila, I'll wash the blackboards." But they ignored me and doted on Angelique, making a big fuss about her red hair and green eyes.*

They ignored me even though I excelled in arithmetic. But did the nuns care? No, they only raved about how good Angelique was at writing. Only sweet Sister Agnes cared. Of course, my parents didn't have the money 'the great goddess Angelique's' parents had. I mean who can compete with the Rockefeller and Astor coffers?

Mr. Hoover in middle school saved me. He saw my way with snakes, how they loved me when no one else did. How I loved them. How I could get any snake to

[29]

wind around my arm. Angelique tried, but they knew she was a fraud. One even bit her—not a poisonous one, though. After that she was wary of snakes. But I wasn't. Knowing how good I was with snakes, Mr. Hoover taught me how to work with them.

Even after being excluded by Angelique and her clique in grammar school, *I tried to be part of her crowd in high school, but she ignored me then, too. I read once that being ignored is worse than being bullied because at least when you're bullied, you're noticed. I wasn't noticed. I was invisible.*

When the play Chicago *came out, the kids in high school started calling me 'cellophane Jane.' The nickname stuck. Someone even wrote a parody of the lyrics in my school annual, right under my picture. That hurt.*

"Here's to cellophane Jane, the girl you can look right through and walk right by and never know she's there."

I never forgot that. Well, my snakes know I'm here. And they love me, and I love them.

Chapter Six

Toward the conclusion of our High Tea when the conversation began to ebb a little, Angelique declared, "For those of you who have no prior obligations and are able to stay a bit longer, I'd love to share my latest collection."

"What are you collecting these days, Angelique?" Hanaka asked, inferring Angelique had many collections—or at least started many.

"Isabella Fayette's."

"Isabella Fayette as in Isabella Fayette's purses?" I asked.

"Exactly the one, Elizabeth. Do you know her work? She's from Milan, you know."

"Yes, Duarte gave me three, actually four, of her *minaudières* over the course of our marriage. I understand now they are considered more jewelry than accessory."

"Which ones do you have, Darling?"

I ticked them off, "The vintage penguin—one of her earliest. The rose, in red—not the pink one. My favorite—the white beaded and crystal polar bear."

"Oh, Darling, I covet the polar bear," remarked Angelique. "It's impossible to find him these days. But why did you say four when you only enumerated three?"

[31]

"Du had also gotten me the pug-faced golden dog with its pill box match inside, but it was stolen when our home was broken into years ago. I never replaced it."

"Why not?"

"Long story."

"I hate to appear *gauche*, Girls," Cathy interrupted, but quite honestly I'm clueless—Isabella Fayette?"

Hanaka immediately spoke up, "My family personally knew Isabelle. She was a Hungarian American fashion designer who fled the Nazis and brought her luxurious but unusually shaped *minaudières* to the world."

Cathy shaped her mouth in an *O*.

"I'm lucky enough to own her 'Diamond Flawless Crystal Clutch,' Hanaka continued, "my husband gave it to me when he proposed. It looks like a gigantic diamond with a geometric pattern of crystals and brass." Hanaka brought her hands together to fashion a bowl shape. "I treasure it. I understand there are many collectors of Fayette's crystalline handbags. One woman in New Orleans claims to own fifty Fayette's."

"That collection must be worth a fortune," gasped Angelique.

"Probably multiples over six-digits," Hanaka stated rather matter-of-factly.

[32]

I mentally calculated the worth of my three pieces—*Not bad, Du, not a bad investment at all,* I thought, *not that I'd ever sell them.*

Angelique said, "The First Lady carried one for the inaugural. She fancied them. It was her loyalty to Texas and to Neiman-Marcus, I think. As a matter of fact, you can see some of Fayette's whimsical designs displayed at the Bush Presidential Library and Museum."

"One of the early episodes of *Sex and the City* featured Carrie carrying to a cocktail party the absolutely gorgeous Fayette that Big had just given her," I said.

"I remember that episode," chimed in Hanaka.

I added "If you looked closely throughout that episode, you'd notice several other women carrying classic Fayette's, too." Then I thought about Hanaka's dark glasses and worried I had blundered by using words like *looked closely* and *notice.*

Ignoring my possible *faux pas,* the ever impatient, Cathy said, "Well, Angelique, do show us *your* collection." *Thank you, Cathy. Your impetuosity help smooth what could have been an awkward situation,* I thought.

"Several of my pieces are still under lock and key in storage at my mountain home. There's a carpenter fellow in Pennsylvania that specializes in designing unbreakable glass cabinets to fit your decor. I've ordered several made with singular locks to display all my pieces here, so you must come back to see the full collection when that those cases are installed. But I'll happily show you what I have on hand here at home right now."

With that Angelique led us to a small study where she retrieved a wooden box lined with foam from a closet. With the care of a curator handling an ancient artifact, she took out six pieces all wrapped in a soft material worthy of a designer gown. Placing them carefully on her cocktail table, she positioned herself on the carpet, cross-legged in front of the table like an elementary school student. I thought, *now that's being in shape. I wonder how long she is able to sit like that at her age. I guess exercise pays off.* Meanwhile, Angelique had unwrapped each minaudièrein turn. We all leaned toward the table. She identified each piece by name or context or both for our benefit.

"This is a fun one," she began, holding it like an iPhone. "It's called, 'Call Me Back.' My children gifted it to me last Christmas for obvious reasons. They claim I'm on the phone far too much."

We all examined a purse that accurately resembled an iPhone. Its cord served as the purse's lanyard. I loved it. Immediately, we all wanted one.

"This all beaded one is called 'Martini Glass Cocktail Clutch.' The girls in my book club gave it to me years ago because I used to love martinis so much." We all tittered appropriately. "Just look at its details: the

[34]

stem of the glass, even the olive—resembles the real thing, doesn't it? Don't you want to take a bite of that olive and a sip of the martini?"

We all laughed. I quipped, "Now that you moved to Cosmopolitans, Angelique, you need to get one titled 'Cosmos.'" More titters.

Lifting the next purse out of the box almost lovingly, Angelique said with a faraway look in her eyes, "When we bought our home at the Jersey shore, my husband gave me this Fayette, 'Ocean's Conch Shell,' so we named our home 'Forester's Conch Shell.' We even had a sign fashioned in the shape of a conch shell that we hung over the front door. I adore this piece for sentimental reasons. That turned out to be an extraordinary summer. You might remember, Girls, it was the summer Nixon resigned. I almost never carry it, though, as it makes me weep for the sand and surf and all the fun we had at our shore home in the past."

I bet Angelique is thinking of her deceased husband, crossed my mind. Then she added, "I fear those times are gone forever."

None of us knew what to say to that, so in the uncomfortable silence that followed the word *forever,* Angelique picked up another piece.

"'Rocking Horse Penelope' celebrates the birth of our only daughter—named Penelope, of course. This one is so dear to me." She then clutched it to her chest to reinforce her words.

[35]

"I love them all," Cathy said. "Anytime you want to share your collection, just let me know."

Even though Angelique is a generous soul, that's probably *not likely to happen,* I thought.

"I have one more here. It's the famous 'Swarovski Crystal Pistol.'"

"OMG!" said Franny, who rarely said anything. "That looks exactly like the miniature pistol my mother used to carry in her purse for safety's sake."

"Fayette is known for the accuracy of her concepts. I rather favor this one, too. It's a limited edition, so it's worth just steadily climbs. I have my eye on more of Fayette's designs, too. As I told you, I also have a few in storage, but these are my most cherished ones thus far," Angelique concluded.

We all gushed appropriately and called out our favorites and why, and asked if and where they might be purchased. She elaborated more on each piece. I could tell our comments and reactions pleased Angelique. She liked that we were involved—the goal of any hostess. It proved to be a fine, fine High Tea, interesting and informative, all the way around.

"Do call me when you return from Scotland, Darling," Angelique whispered in my ear as she hugged me good-bye. "We'll have much to discuss as Scotland is one of my favorite places in the world. And good luck with your new forensic fellow. He sounds utterly charming. I can't wait to meet him. You simply must bring him round sometime."

Once outside, the doorman hailed me a cab but not before Cathy pulled me aside and said in a stage whisper, "It's apparent, Elizabeth, you don't know."

"Don't know what?"

"Hanaka is almost blind!"

"What? Why? Does everyone know?"

"No, only a few of us are privy to this, but Hanaka's devastated. I heard she even tried to commit *harakiri*."

"Oh, no! How did this happen?"

"I'll text you," she said as her cab drove up followed by another—mine. "I'll text you later this evening."

"Please do," I said as she jumped into the cab.

**Chapter Seven**

"How was High Tea?" Aladar asked as I entered our kitchen and raised my lips to his. "I missed you," he said, as he kissed me long and lingeringly.

"I thought of you," I said, holding him in a hug.

"You did?" he asked.

"Yes, when Angelique showed us her spectacular shower with the slatted built-in seat."

"Are you tempting me?" Aladar asked.

"Of course. Shall I cease and desist?"

"Of course not. Where's the fun in that? I want to hear more about that shower, but first tell me about your afternoon."

That's when I noticed Aladar had prepared our favorite cocktails and placed them side-by-side on what looked like hand-printed menus. Obviously, he was eager to share what he had devised.

"What's this?" I asked, pointing with one elbow to the menus, my arms still around him.

"Read one," he suggested, "out loud—on the sofa."

As I began, Aladar nestled in, resting his arm comfortably around my shoulders like a warm fur muffler. He began snogging my neck.

"My goodness, Aladar, I was only gone for the afternoon!"

"I told you I missed you."
I began to read aloud:

"Menu:

Appetizers—choose one to do after the lights dim
  *Slow dancing to some romantic music
  *Repeated kissing but above the neck only
  *A few minutes of tactilely getting re-acquainted
  (see forensic journal for refresher on the meaning)
Main course—choose one
  *Vietnamese take out, must be eaten on the
carpet in casual attire
  *Italian at our favorite restaurant down the street

  *Grazing off whatever we find in the fridge and
pantry
Dessert—choose one
  *Smooching on the sofa
  *Watching a movie on TV
  *Taking Coco for a walk
Digestif—choose one
      *Grappa
      *Amaro
      *Sambuca
      *Pacharán
  Sweets—choose one
      *Strawberries dipped in chocolate
      *Gelato
      *Fruit macaroons
  Nobbling"

"This is a new tactic you've created here, Aladar. How does it work?"

"You vote in secret, and I vote in secret. We then compare votes. If we agree, we do what we agreed upon. If we don't agree, we discuss options. Sound fair?"

"Sounds fair and fun. Do I see two copies of the menu?"

"Yes, you do. Each copy provides the coasters for our drinks."

"You thought of everything. No peeking as I choose," I warned, slipping my menu out from under its glass and grabbing a nearby pencil.

As it turns out, I voted for slow dancing. Aladar voted for repeated kissing above the neck. We compromised with the tactilely getting re-acquainted.

We both voted for Vietnamese for the main course, and we both wanted to watch a movie afterwards.

I voted for Pacharán but Aladar chose Grappa.

We both wanted Gelato. That left nobbling.

"Aladar, my definition of *nobbling* is rather negative. One meaning is a synonym for stealing. The other is somewhat naughty. What was that your intention?"

To my surprise Aladar said, "Stealing."

"What are we stealing?"

"Each other's hearts."

[40]

Now that's an aah, I thought but I asked, "How is that supposed to happen?"

"The idea is a word game. We use our persuasive verbal arsenal to convince the other person to do what we want. In this case, not so much by force or incapacitating but through the power of words. Are you in?"

"Do birds fly? You know I love word games. But you begin."

"My purpose is to charm you into the bedroom. I intend to abduct you."

"Silly boy. That is far too direct. I refuse." I countered.

"Methinks you are merely glozing. You really want to join me in the bedroom," Aladar said.

"Me thinks you think incorrectly," I said.

"How might I convince you nobbling is a good thing?" he said.

"You could try blandishment." I said.

"Don't you mean banishment?" he asked, getting lost in his own game.

"No. I suggested blandishment." I repeated the word more distinctly.

"All by itself?" he asked.

"Well, a bit of cuddling along with the words might be in order."

"You win," he said. "I'll work on that."

[41]

Aladar reached over and turned the light from dim to dimmer. It was the perfect ending to a perfect day—a re-uniting with old friends and a re-uniting with the man I was quite sure I was falling in love with and who loved me.

"By the way, Aladar, to answer your question," I whispered, "High Tea was quite nice. I'll tell you all about it and that shower in the morning." Just then my phone signaled a text.

"Oh, Aladar, that's Cathy. She had some news for me, but our cabs came before she could tell me, so she said she'd text me. That's her text."

"I'm sure it can wait," Aladar said with just a hint of annoyance in his voice.

"I'm not so sure it can," I said, "Hanaka Haruki is going blind. It's heartbreaking. Let me check." Sighing a deep sigh of resignation, but an even deeper sigh of understanding, Aladar turned in the sofa, grabbed his grappa, and motioned for me to go ahead.

Cathy's message was brief: "Can you call me?"

I quickly punched in her number. She picked up even more quickly.

"What is going on?" I asked without preamble.

"Our dear classmate is almost totally blind now but will soon become totally blind. She's deeply depressed."

"When did this happen?"

"We started noticing it about a month or so ago. She tried to keep it quiet for a while, but we kept asking about her sour moods since they were so uncharacteristic, so she finally told us. You were wrapped up in the wedding plans and your trip to Scotland, so we didn't tell you. It all started when she went to a Doctor Simi who supposedly specializes in blepharoplasty...."

"What's that?" I interrupted.

"...that's the plastic surgery Asians undergo to create an eyelid crease. They want their Asian eyes to look more like ours, more like what they call 'westernized,'" Cathy explained.

"So, what happened?"

"Hanaka went to this Doctor Simi, known for this surgery on mono-lids, but he slipped; that's what happened. Skilled surgeon that he is, somehow the knife slipped. He's claiming his knife, the one made expressly for his hand, was switched somehow. He told Hanaka's attorney that it didn't feel right in his hand from the beginning, but he went along with the procedure anyway since she was prepped, and the room readied and all that." *I thought about a previous case Aladar and I worked—Reggie, knives, numbers on knives, precision of the handles...* Cathy was still talking, "Naturally, there's a big lawsuit involved, but she's devastated. Keeps talking about wanting to die, more specifically to kill herself."

[43]

"How awful. Is there anything we can do?"

"I'm not sure. But I should know more by the time you get back from Scotland. Actually, I was surprised she attended Angelique's pre-reunion. She's so severely depressed, she doesn't go out much now. Didn't you notice any difference in her?"

"Outside of the dark glasses?"

"Well, yes. They are off putting, aren't they?"

"I'm not sure I'd call them off putting so much as distracting. I'm ashamed to admit that besides those glasses, I didn't observe much that was different about her. So much is happening in my life, and I was so excited to see the five of you, I'm afraid I was oblivious."

"You're excused, Elizabeth, but do stay in touch."

My mind had strayed back to Aladar and that sweet word game we were playing before Cathy called. In the middle of my absentmindedness that probably produced a lull in the conversation, Cathy said, "Well, I better go. Thanks for calling. I thought you should know."

"Thanks for telling me. I'll be in touch."

"Have fun in Scotland. Drink some scotch for me."

"Will do."

[44]

Chapter Eight

"The fabrics have arrived" enthused Pheme into the phone. "Do come over, Grand Auntie. They are positively the most beautiful materials ever! We have them all displayed at Grammy's."

Knowing Pheme as the master of hyperbole, I usually questioned her use of superlatives, but since we were talking about 'The House of Chanel,' I was curious to see what had arrived. I rushed next door, grabbing Coco on the way. Coco loved being around anything social, so I knew she would jump and dance about on her hind legs in the rhythm of our reactions to the luxuriant materials.

Greeting me were fabrics in every shade of white—from cream and ecru to powder and pearl. The English professor in me loved the names given to the different shades, each clearly meant to evoke a different response—*great lesson on lexicon,* I thought as I read the labels: milk, coconut, parchment, feather, swan, porcelain, cupcake, frost.

Spread out on sofas, chairs, over tables, and on sideboards, an array of lovely silks, gossamers, satins, chiffons, crepes, laces, velvets, and embroidered fabrics partially or totally unrolled were displayed. Swatches of other samples lay everywhere.

[45]

I noticed Glady had already chosen the color "bubbles." I was sure she had chosen it because it held just the most delicate touch of a seafoam green being cheerful without being too cool a color and not being hospital white.

"Cascading white," her other choice, roughly approximated the color of a waterfall, its texture that of a waterfall. The accent—I could see it as Glady's veil. I was certain she had the seas of Scotland and its white heather in mind when choosing both "whites."

Glady had already ordered her wedding gown— a challenge to be perfect, to be sure—but one worth the research she had done. Designed in the house of Chanel by Stella Van Jen, Gladys requested a high scalloped neck with slender cuffed sleeves and a classic silhouette that would hug her bodice in the most flattering way. The fabric would be the finest *peau de soie* and lace. As she pondered over the buttons, I thought, *will she ever decide?* But her taste was undeniably stunning, perhaps because she took her time. The open back would be accentuated with illusion tulle. She had also requested a modified ruffled hemline with an abbreviated train.

"I don't want to be dragging a long, heavy train around the castle grounds," Glady confided. "I love long trains that go on for miles, but not for me and not for the glens of Scotland."

[46]

The bridesmaids had chosen the most becoming A-line tiered gowns with scoop necklines and ankle-length hemlines. Interestingly, the soft silk material we all picked held a hint of a floral outline (a nod to Grammy) without an ostentatious floral pattern. Kenneth Avery, also within the house of Chanel, had designed our gowns with the foresight of our different figures in mind—especially Pheme's, who was barely showing now, but who would be 'farther along,' for the first fitting and even farther along for the wedding itself.

Avery's aim was to have us all look stylish yet classic in what we chose. I loved my gown and hoped to be able to wear it again—*maybe to that 65th reunion, I thought.* I couldn't wait for those fittings.

As for the men, Glady insisted they be attired in full formal Scottish wear. Although they grumbled, they succumbed to being measured for tuxedoes with tails, single breasted with peak lapels and grey, three-button waistcoats. They would also wear tartan kilts in the plaid of Dr. Henson's ancestral pattern. White dress shirts, bow ties, top hats, gloves, and dress shoes would complete their look.

I thought, *Aladar will look particularly smashing and sexy in his top hat* and those kilts!

 **Chapter Nine**

In the middle of all these fabrics and fantasies, Angelique called. I hoped I didn't register surprise when I answered, but I honestly wasn't expecting to hear from her since she had asked me at the end of the tea to call her when I returned from Scotland. *This must be urgent,* I reasoned. I was right. She sounded anguished.

"Darling, I realize you're knee deep in your sister's wedding, but I'm beside myself."

"What's the problem. Angelique?"

"I received a most mysterious and worrisome note. Apparently, someone passed it to our doorman, who doesn't remember anything about who gave it to him. He claims it was slipped to him just as some folks arrived, so he was distracted with their luggage and such. All he remembers is the person saying, "Make sure you give this to Angelique Forester."

"What does the note say?"

Life isn't fair. I'm going to kill you.

"Oh, my! That's it?"

"That's it. That's enough! Do you think your forensic investigator friend could give it a look? Maybe there are fingerprints he could check or something I am missing," Angelique's voice kept rising in tandem with her anxiety.

"I'll be happy to ask him. When may he call you?"

"Any time. Quite frankly, I'm terrified. There has been such a rise in crime of late..." she
trailed off.

I thought of what the cabbie had said, *But tell your friend to be extrey careful. There's been more activity, if youse get my drift, up that way lately. Word on the street is the mob is prowlin' for someone, revenge thing, makes it risky for everybody, if youse get my drift.*

"Try to stay calm, Angelique. Dr. Aladar Gallant is an expert. If there's anything to be found in or on that note, he's your man." With that, we hung up. I immediately called Aladar.

# Chapter Ten

"Sure. I'll be happy to help Angelique out. We have a team here trained in examining documents, Elizabeth."

"She'll be relieved to hear that, Aladar. "

"These people systematically inspect and compare documents using specific standards. They can determine the nature and even the source of the paper and sometimes even of the writing and printing."

"I learn each day more and more about your work," I admitted. "Frankly, Aladar, after our investigation in and around that Castalanno case we worked and solved a while ago, I'm awed."

"Let me see how backed up the team is, and I'll call you on a time." Aladar said but not before I heard the pleasure of receiving that compliment in his voice.

"Good. Then I'll hold off giving Angeliquea specific time for us to meet until I hear from you."

I barely returned to the fabrics and the orderly confusion that characterized my life of late, when Aladar called back.

"Elizabeth, the team is excited about this. It seems there's been a lot of crime uncharacteristically in that area of the City lately, so they are eager to help out all they can. Will you set up a meeting with Angelique?"

"Happy to do so."

[50]

Aladar, along with his team of forensic specialists, Angelique, and I met at her place soon after Aladar's call. Angelique produced the note the doorman had given her. Aladar received it with a gloved hand and immediately placed it in a plastic bag. "We'll closely examine this ASAP," Aladar assured her.

I must admit this second visit to Angelique's impressed me just as much as did the first visit. *Unlike so many places in the City that are small and dark, hers is spacious, light and bright, a place to be happy,* I thought, when *not saddled with such a threatening note.*

She had decided we'd be able to spread out any documents or equipment and be more comfortable in the dining area, so that's where she led us.

"I had Mary, my domestic prepare us some tidbits for munching as we work," Angelique explained as we walked to the dining area. There we were treated to her idea of "tidbits." Laid before us was everything from nuts to popcorn, from snack crackers to about four different cheeses, from lunch meats and breads to mini corn dogs, from cookies to cupcakes. We also had our choice of teas, coffee, soft drinks, and imported water in tiny bottles.

"Thank you, Angelique," Aladar said, "but we really didn't expect such a treat."

"Everyone works better on a full tummy," came the gracious replay. *Angelique was nothing if not*

[51]

gracious, I thought. With those amenities out of the way, we got down to work.

We began with the paper. The forensic examiners and Aladar began testing the color, thickness, weight, and weave pattern. They conducted a fiber analysis. I watched, fascinated. They used paper calipers for measuring and a small but sensitive scale, which they had brought with them, for weighing. Then they cut a tiny piece from the note and disintegrated it in water.

They also examined the watermark. "This allows us to determine the manufacture and date of production, which often proves helpful," Aladar explained. Several minutes later he reported, "Angelique, the note you received was written on a top-quality paper, probably recently purchased at Saks or Bloomingdales or directly from the company that calls itself, 'Dear Annabelle.' It's a highly distinctive line, therefore, it was easy for us to identify."

The watermark proved interesting because it was created by whomever bought this paper.

"Individuals can add their own custom watermarks," Aladar said.

"I didn't know that," I said.

"Yes, it's common among those wanting something unique. Making your own ensures uniqueness while screaming "creative" (and money) to the recipient."

[52]

"Why did you soak that tiny piece of the stationery in water?" Angelique asked no one in particular.

One of the team members answered, "This high-quality stationary contains more than the average amount of wood fiber. In order to identify paper of this type, we had to cut a small piece to use for analysis."

"So, this note was written on expensive stationery?" Angelique asked.

"The best. I have never in all my years in forensics seen paper any finer. That, of course, gives us some valuable information. Now on to the inks. You may be interested to know, Ms. Forester, that we have a data base of almost 10,000 inks. We call it our 'Ink Library. Not incidentally, it is maintained by the Secret Service. This resource allows us to compare the composition of different inks."

"Why, I had no idea," exclaimed Angelique grasping the antique broach she had pinned to her lapel."

That singular act forced me to look at her broach. Even from across the table, I could see its tiny pen shape encrusted with diamonds. From where I sat it looked as if the pen's point was a single onyx, giving the impression that the pen was filled with ink and ready to write. *What I would give to own that piece,* the writer in me thought.

A different member of the team was explaining inks to Angelique, "Ms. Forester, just as the paper used for this note is of the highest quality, so is the ink. We determined it's Faber-Castell, one of the highest quality inks in the world. In the forensic world we love it because it is indelible, smudge-resistant, reproducible, and waterproof. What helps us in our work is that Faber-Castell cannot be erased and is resistant to solvents."

"I had no idea there was so much to this."

"When we see this quality of ink, we don't have to go any farther to ascertain if more was written or if anything had been expunged." He turned to all of us, adding, "We know that what we see is what we got— nothing less."

At this point, we took a break. The forensic team gathered around me kibitzing, "With these results, we expect the writing utensil to be the famous 'Aurora Diamante."

"Tell me about that pen," I prodded. I had heard of it, but never actually saw one.

"For starters," one fellow on the team said, "it's valued at a cool $1.4 million. As a joke, I once told my wife I wanted one for Christmas. She bit, even wrote down the name. Told me something like, 'Well, maybe Santa will be good to you.' But after she priced it, she told me I was going to get 'coal and wood' for baiting her like that. She has no sense of humor."

[54]

"What makes that pen so expensive?" I asked, prudently avoiding his wife's foibles.

"Thirty carats of diamonds and it's solid platinum!"

"But not just *any* diamonds," a colleague interjected, "those are the famous De Beers diamonds!"

"Oh, I'm sure Dr. Gallant has that on his Christmas list for each of you!" I said obviously with tongue in cheek.

Loud guffaws followed my remark. Boisterous expressions: "I wish," "If only," "Now, that would be some Christmas present!" trailed along like lingering sounds of a bell.

"We may dream and kid around, but actually we have discovered something telling about the writer of that note." Aladar said, "he or she, most likely a she (but we've yet to determine that) is either quite wealthy or has purloined that stationery and ink. Tells me more about the message, too." Aladar said.

"How so, Dr. Gallant?" someone asked.

"Usually, it's *not* our wealthy neighbors who complain about the unfairness of life."

[55]

# Chapter Eleven

"What will happen next, Dr. Gallant?" Angelique asked.

"Without boring you too much with details, let me just tell you that this note will be scrutinized using ACE-V Methodology."

"What is that?" both Angelique and I asked simultaneously.

"It's an acronym for Analysis, Comparison, Evaluation, and Verification, thus—ACE-V—for short. Scientists are fond of acronyms."

"As are English professors," I added, smiling.

"So, is this ACE-V a way to examine this note in depth?" Angelique pressed.

"Precisely. But even after the first ACE-V is completed, a second expert retests the original hypothesis using ACE-V once again to catch anything missed."

I turned to Aladar, "Sounds like a version of abductive reasoning, does it not—formulating then testing and retesting a hypothesis?"

Aladar nodded. He continued, "I'm not certain handwriting will help us, but our experts will continue to examine the paper, ink, watermarks, markings, anything altered, even disturbed paper fibers before we tackle the handwriting."

"My goodness," Angelique muttered, "I had no idea, no idea," she kept repeating.

"We'll find everything if there's anything to find," Aladar assured her. "Give us a few days."

With that I stood as did Angelique and Aladar. There was a pause, then another. Then Angelique said, "There *is* something else."

"Ah, and what might that be?" I just stared at Angelique, astonished that she had been holding something back from us.

"One of my minaudière's has gone missing."

"An Isabella Fayette?" I asked.

"No, one even more valuable, if you can imagine. One I did not show the group, which makes its disappearance even more troublesome. It's an original Fabergé."

Aladar listened to all this with interest, then he suggested, "We need to process all this. I have an idea. Let's jump into a cab and grab a drink at Chapel Bar, which isn't that far from here. They serve wonderful cocktails made from recipes that date back to the Roman days, and it's quiet enough for us to continue this conversation. Besides, I'm a Fotografiska Museum patron, so we'll have no trouble securing a table. I've been wanting to impress Elizabeth by taking her there. This seems to be a good time."

"I vote yes," I said immediately, thinking, *I've long wanted to visit that 19th Century Chapel, that sanctuary of culture morphed into a ritzy contemporary bar.*

"I'll echo Elizabeth," said Angelique. "Did you know Chapel Bar was featured on that Netflix show *Inventing Anna?*"

"No, but that's all the more reason to have a drink there," I said, adding, "given that we, too, are on a quest."

"So off we go," said Aladar.

"I'm surprised you were never there," Aladar whispered in my ear as we climbed into the taxi, "You're going to love it."

I did. I could have just wallowed for hours in the vibes from that old Church Mission House or the spirits created by monks and priests both real and fictional. Mysterious, the bar's dark sophisticated space provided us with the perfect gathering place. Aladar was right. I loved it!

The Chapel Bar struck me as the quintessential setting for what Angelique told us next, located in a space that was formerly a cathedral. The high ceilings and massive chandelier invited quiet conversation. The entire experience seemed a bit like confession. We sat in a small dark anteroom in armchairs. I felt like a member of some secret society.

"This is spectacular, Aladar. More—It's downright sensuous," I murmured.

Angelique gushed, "These colors—amethyst booths and emerald pillows with citrine light fixtures just make the photography on the walls look bejeweled. No place could fit our purpose for being here better!"

"Here comes the drink menu," Aladar announced, "get ready."

The drinks, at least the specialty drinks, were in Roman numerals! The menu also explained that we could find the Chartreuse, made by Carthusian monks since 1737, in several of the cocktails. Other monastic nods on the unconventional menu were given to the Benedictines and of course the often-regaled Dom Pierre Perignon for inventing Champagne back in 1697. *If I were writing a novel right now,* I thought, *this is where I'd place an important conversation.*

**Chapter Twelve**

After we ordered and took several sips of these exotic drinks, ending with contented sighs, Aladar turned his attention to Angelique, "What is the other news you have?"

"As I told Elizabeth, since our college pre-union gathering, one of my minaudières has gone missing."

"I take it, this one is quite valuable—maybe more so than the others?"

"Oh, yes, probably the most valuable of all my pieces. It's a Fabergé, so it's one of the earliest created minaudières. Supposedly the idea came to Peter Carl Fabergé, who was a Russian Jeweler, when he saw a woman of stature put some coins into a small metal box she was carrying."

"Really? I didn't know that," I said.

"Mine was—I mean—is egg-shaped—you know Fabergé is known for that shape. It has beautifully detailed lilies of the valley cascading around it."

"What's its value?" Aladar prodded.

"Close to six figures."

We sat for several minutes in silence allowing that information to infiltrate our brains and the warmth of the drinks to permeate our bodies.

"Do you have any suspects in mind?" I asked Angelique.

[60]

"Not really, but I'm wondering if the culprit responsible for that horrid note is also responsible for the theft."

"Likely," Aldar admitted.

"Who would have access?" I asked. "Your place seems so secure."

"Well, the doorman for one." Angelique said. "Then, I guess any of the workers who executed my custom kitchen designs, but that was several months ago. There's Mary, my domestic, plus Jane, the laundress." Turning to me, Angelique asked as if the idea just occurred to her, "Should I include the 'Girls' I invited for that pre-reunion high tea as suspects?"

"I would think anyone who recently visited your place should be considered." *although I cannot imagine why one of us would steal anything, or even* how *one of us could do that,* rolled across my brain.

With that speculation and with our last sip of Roman I, we left this fabulous posh place and headed home.

Our taxi dropped off Angelique first, and we waited until she was well inside the building. I didn't see her doorman, though, and wondered about that.

# Chapter Thirteen

"What an unexpectedly interesting day!" I exclaimed as Aldar encircled my waist and kissed me once we were inside the door.

"Shall we top it off with an unexpectedly interesting night?" Aladar rejoined.

"Why not?"

Just then my phone pinged.

"Hi Ande, what's up?"

"Grammy has decided we shall all travel to Scotland this weekend. Pack your duds; the plane and pilots stand ready."

"What? Why a week ahead of schedule?"

"I'm not sure, but I'm stoked about this wedding, so I rather like the idea of leaving early. Grammy has all kinds of things planned—investigating other castles, touring museums, visiting distilleries, as well as taking that side trip to Paris, not to exclude that glam wedding itself and the reception in her very own castle. So, as I said, pack your duds."

"Oh dear! Aladar and I just got entangled in a new case."

"Grand Auntie, be real! Your ninety-three-year-old sister is getting married in Scotland; she'll become a Viscountess! Everything else can wait."

"You're so right, Ande."

I hung up and turned to Aladar, who picked up a word here and there and had inferred the meaning of it all.

"I have to agree with Ande," he said. "Let's pack our bags!"

"Not until I call Angelique."

**Chapter Fourteen**

"Yes, Angelique, I am off to Scotland for a month or so. My older, richer-than-god sister is getting married and it's to be quite an extravaganza. Besides, I'm in the bridal party, and as a member of the family, I can't renege—*not that I want to*—we are all being flown to Edinburgh with a side trip to Paris. I simply cannot bow out."

"Of course, Darling, I understand, but promise you'll call me the minute you touch back on American soil."

"I promise. In the meantime, don't do anything foolish. I don't want to frighten you, but you could be in danger."

"Oh, Elizabeth, I'm an old-time New Yorker. We don't scare easily. We are made of 'sterner stuff,' to quote the Bard."

"I know that, but even a crusty New York City taxi driver issued me a warning the other day. These are dangerous times and you *did* get that note."

"Silly girl. I promise to behave; you have fun in Scotland. Drink the whiskey, inhale the charm, be sure to eat some *haggis*, enjoy yourself, and we'll straighten out all this note business when you return." *Again, the ever-gracious Angelique,* I thought. Little did she or I know what awaited us.

**Chapter Fifteen**

My Beloved Du,

I can only describe the plane trip to Edinburgh as a contemporary airplane version of the old I LOVE LUCY film The Long Long Trailer! *While it was fun to be with the family, the entire trip turned into an eight-hour raucous nightmare on the plane.*

The twins were fitful. One of us had to hold one or the other of them the entire trip. Poor Pheme was exhausted as was Russ. The rest of us tried our best, but nothing worked until Aladar got the brainstorm to play the karaoke music. Good thinking on Pheme's part for packing it. Did you ever? That clamed them down and they finally slept.

Coco proved to be a good traveler, but only when she could sit between Aladar and me. No one else would do. We were hog tied to our seats by our own dog.

Ande got air sick, really air sick. That surprised me given her sophistication, and Boris was no help whatsoever. He's much better managing business than tending to an upchucking wife.

Loraine, we found out too late, had never flown. She sat the entire trip in sheer terror, mostly clutching Sea, terrified the entire time. I could see her white knuckles from across the aisle.

That was when the flight went smoothly. When we hit turbulence, almost everyone panicked. One of the overheads erupted with several pieces of the smaller luggage falling out and opening in the fall. We had lingerie everywhere. That, in itself, was quite a sight. Although panties on Coco's head did provide us with something to laugh about at least for a few minutes. I daresay that part of the trip will become a staple in future family stories.

Grammy slept the entire trip. As usual, nothing upsets her. I was fine with my vodka as was Aladar with his gin.

Perla and Joyce Elizabeth stayed glued to the windows. Just being on an airplane for the first time in their lives proved excitement enough for them. Jadwiga and Wald, who had flown before all the way from Poland, thumbed through the magazines. They were, as the kids say, 'cool.'

Bridget stayed in her seat with a perpetual smile. She couldn't wait to see her family, friends, and her country again. It was like if she stayed in her seat, we would arrive there more quickly—you know, that Irish magical thinking.

As we approached Edinburgh, we hit a bumpy patch. Poor, poor Ande. Even poorer Boris. All in all, we were grateful to land.

But Du, it's soooooo beautiful here. It's sooooo green.

Until next time...

Chapter Sixteen

"Here we were at the castle!" I announced as if no one else could see the imposing stone structure in front of us. We had driven to what was once called 'Maryburgh,' named after Queen Mary II, but we eventually arrived at what is presently called Fort William.

Inverlochy Castle sits at the mouth of the River Lochy. It's commanding, even now in its somewhat partially tumbled down state. Landward, we drove through Glen Spean and the Great Glen, but Glady promised us all another trip via water, so we could approach the castle through Loch Linnhe, which she claims is a totally different and 'must-do' experience.

"The main accommodations at one time," Dr. Henson told us as he pointed toward them, "were in those four towers." Following his point, we could see remnants of the round edifices at three corners of the grounds. Clearly, the fourth one had been recently restored.

Pointing more specifically to it, Dr. Henson said, "The wedding will take place in that north-west corner tower, which is the largest tower and the one in the best condition." He apologized. "I'm sorry I couldn't have all the renovations completed in time for the wedding."

"I wanted all the atmosphere, pomp and glamour we could conjure out of these stones," Gladys followed up with a chuckle. "I have grand plans." She smiled at Dr. Henson; he smiled back. None of us doubted her—or him. She continued, "The other towers

[68]

are under construction as Dr. Henson intends. We both want to restore this castle to its original grandeur eventually. We can see all the possibilities. Then you all must visit again."

"Look at those ruins," Boris said as he called our attention to immense stones near one tower. Considering this castle was built in the 1200s, even the ruins struck us as impressive.

"And look at how thick those walls are!" Russ added, "I can see they formed a quadrangular wall." *Leave it to our numbers man to notice that,* I thought.

Pheme remarked on the wide moat surrounding three sides of the castle, and from her research, she explained why they had moats.

I noticed the two opposing entrance gates. We were all a picture of awe at one thing and then another. If someone had snapped a photo of us at that moment, I'm quite sure, we'd all haveour mouths agape.

"Actually, though," Dr. Henson said, "We will all stay in the new Inverlochy Castle, which is more chateau than castle," gesturing in its direction. "It's a luxury hotel and restaurant with fine dining, afternoon tea (of course) and, it's close to the original castle, as you can see for yourselves by its proximity to where we are presently standing."

I was happy to hear that. Dr. Henson's castle, while romantic and historic, emanating all the loveliness of a medieval romance, looked cold and forbidding to my American eyes, eyes accustomed to all the amenities and conveniences of modern-day living. And by his own admission, Dr. Henson had not yet installed the central heating he had planned. Even in July, walking into those

[69]

castle rooms felt like falling into a freezer. It seemed as if all that masonry held in the cold from the winter months. Even coming from the Northeast, I was not used to that kind of chill.

"I don't care if it looks a bit scary or feels cold," Pheme, our perpetual optimist, said. "I want to read the ghost story in its donjon. They sometimes call it a 'keep.' "It will be a great setting for the story! We can wear jumpers if we're chilly."

"Jumpers, Pheme, really?" asked Loraine.

"*Jumpers* is the Scottish word for sweaters, Loraine," Pheme explained without a hint of condescension in her voice. "And imagine, we're going to be here for almost an entire month! Yay July!" Pheme could hardly contain herself. "We'll find an accommodating time for the story. I know we will."

If I was the family 'writer,' clearly Pheme was its 'storyteller.' She couldn't wait to tell the story of Inverlochy to all the guests.

That night as Aladar and I snuggled under the feather cover, so much the staple in Europe, I said, "I think some of the Scottish words interesting, like *jumpers*."

As we snuggled deeper, I added, "Here, they call these covers feather beds, *leabaidh iteach*, but I remember when I was little, people calling them feather ticks. We always used them in the Northeast as covers," I told Aladar. "I loved the softness of the down feathers and the warmth."

"Down feathers?" Aladar asked.

"Yes, the softest feathers found on the belly of a bird. Only these are used for the finest feather beds.

[70]

Mama Zebeta referred to these feather beds as *pierzynas* in her native language, Polish. When we were little, Glady and I loved jumping onto the big billowy softness and bigness of them—they seemed so huge to us then—we pretend all kinds of fairy tales. Now, it seems we are living a fairy tale."

As we burrowed into the cushiony cloud cover like two meerkats burrowing deeper into their habitats, I told Aladar, "At first only the wealthiest people had feather beds; poor folk slept on straw. But eventually feather beds came to the middle class. By then they were considered so valuable they were actually bequeathed to sons and daughters. Imagine that, Aladar!"

When Aladar didn't answer, I turned to look at him. He had fallen asleep. Yes, the feather bed has done its job, making us perfectly warm and comfortably sleepy. *It's no wonder,* I thought, *they morphed into elder down quilts, duvets, and comforters to be used by the rest of the world in due time.*

As Aladar slept, I reminisced. I loved the feel of this *pierzyna*. It made me think thoughts of long ago, of childhood nights, of wishing on the blessed optatek— the Christmas wafer, of imagining I heard Santa Claus and his reindeer on our rooftop, of the wonder of Christmas mornings.

I thought of the twins, of dreaming dreams only the innocent can conjure. I wondered what their lives would be like.

I thought of Grammy and her new road, her new life, her boldness, her acumen.

[71]

This *pierzyna* reminded me of my Polish grandparents, Zebeta and Adam, and how they dared to cross the ocean in search of the promise of a new world, how brave they had been, how fortunate Gladys, Joe, Frank, and I were that they held that daring in their souls. How lucky we were to have Russ and Pheme, Loraine and Sea, Ande and Boris. But how sad we were to have lost Trés.

Then I thought about Du and our fairy tale life together, and finally now how blessed I was to have found Aladar in these twilight years. Then I, too, fell into a deep peaceful sleep.

Chapter Seventeen

We stayed busy, practicing several times at St. Mary's Church. Bastien, the 'Wedding Planner' the House of Chanel had sent to Edinburgh for the duration of the wedding, was a debonair fellow, a stickler for the rules of etiquette, and charming in the way of all things European. He caused the entire wedding party to fall in love with him at once. We were collectively happy to have him overseeing and conducting the rehearsals for the wedding as well as the event itself,

"We must walk the traditional walk," he cautioned at the outset. "We must eat in the style of the Scottish gentry," he admonished as we went along. "We must observe all the intricacies of their world since the wedding is on their soil, "he advised. We acquiesced, complying joyfully as we, too, wanted to become part of this incredible culture, and in spite of our rather prominent social standing in the States, we didn't want to come across as bumpkins in Scotland.

"I understand the good doctor Henson has invited the entire burgh of Fort William for the ceremony and reception," Bastien said. "The Henson family goes back centuries and is held in the highest esteem here. With that in mind, we must be vigilant in all things Scottish."

"Glady has also contracted with the Church of St. Mary's to have its bells ringing before, during, and after the ceremony. Won't that be lovely?" I mentioned.

[73]

Of course, everyone thought. "Of course," everyone said aloud.

"What other specific traditions do you suggest we honor?" Aladar asked Bastien.

Good question, I thought.

"We want Gladys and Dr. Henson to be lucky, so somebody must be designated to hide a spring of white heather in Gladys' bouquet. That ensures good luck and happiness," Bastien answered smiling broadly. *Clearly this chap loves his work,* I thought.

That's an easy one, I thought, *as Gladys told me she made arrangements for white heather to be everywhere. I think her entire bouquet is to be white heather.*

I whispered to Pheme, "I'm reminded of those fairy tales where white heather plays a big part. One I especially loved was about Malvina. When she lost her lover Ossian, who died in battle, she cried so copiously, she turned all the purple heather in Scotland white."

"There was a reason for that," Pheme whispered back. "If I remember that fairy tale, Malvina says something at the end like 'although this white heather symbolizes my sorrow, I want it henceforth to bring good luck to all who find it.' For a long time, I wanted to name any girl child of mine Malvina." I thought, *that's so like Pheme, turning something negative into the positive—even in a fairy tale.*

Ande, overhearing our whispers, added. "Then, of course, there's the classic *Wuthering Heights.* In that novel, Catherine, pure and innately good, is often associated with the flowers of the white heather bush."

[74]

Bastien was still talking, "We are also going to have the Grand March, a procession that begins with the bride and groom marching to the sound of bagpipes, because, of course, we shall have bagpipes?" He changed the pitch of his voice as he tossed us that last question along with a questioning look. We all vigorously nodded. "Then the bride and groom will enjoy the first dance after which others join in."

"Gladys will have a sixpence in her shoe as well as something old, something new, something borrowed, and something blue somewhere on her person," I offered.

"Most especially, though, we'll have the tradition of 'handfasting,'" piped up Pheme.

"What is that?" Boris asked. *Boris must have fallen asleep during that part of Pheme's story*, I thought just a little annoyed at him.

But Bastien was not nonplussed. He continued, "This tradition dates back in Scotland to the 16th and 17th centuries. Tying the hands of the bride and groom together solidifies the a contract. The Scottish term itself roughly translates into the phrase, "to strike a bargain by joining hands."

"I understand now," Boris said. "It's like men shaking hands to close a deal."

Nodding to Boris, Bastien explained further, "A variation of the old Celtic wedding tradition, it's also historically part of all Pagan and Wiccan celebrations, dating back hundreds of years. In fact, handfasting experts say when it first originated, duos needed to wear the ribbon for a year and a day, and then decide if they would like to stay married. If they wanted to

[75]

separate, off came the ribbons; it would be as if they were never married. It was more like a 'trial marriage' than a traditional wedding."

"That's pretty open-minded, if you ask me," said Sea.

"Glady and Dr. Henson intend to use material in the Henderson clan colors as an additional symbol of their unity," I interjected. "They are not going to literally tie a knot but have asked me to lay that swatch of clan-colored material over their hands as the clergyperson officiates their vows."

"How lovely," said Pheme, ever the romantic.

"Then the ceremony will end with everyone singing, "Auld Lang Syne," Bastien concluded.

"The song we sing on New Year's Eve?" Loraine asked.

Bastien said, "Yes, but here we sing it for weddings, too. 'Tis a Scottish poem usually attributed to Rabbie Burns. Reminds us to remember the old and celebrate what is to come."

We were all in with that.

Chapter Eighteen

We returned from rehearsals weary but inspired. The wedding was to be held in two days. We had been in Scotland a little under a month during which time we had visited several castles, many lochs, including Loch Ness(no sign of the monster, though, much to Joyce Elizabeth's disappointment), walked through many cathedrals, took a scenic road trip and a scenic train ride, gone to the Highlands, the Shetland Islands, and Speyside's Malt Whisky Trail. We explored Edinburgh, Glasgow, Inverness, Aberdeen, spent a day at the National Museum of Scotland and another at the Kelvingrove Art Gallery and Museum.

For Joyce Elizabeth's sake we all took the Harry Potter tour which included Hogwarts Castle, Hogwarts Lake, Black Lake, the Quidditch Tournaments, and Hogwarts Express. After all that, everyone wanted to read or re-read all the Harry Potter books!

Aladar insisted on visiting the Edinburgh Gin Distillery while the rest of us were satisfied sipping our way through several scotch whisky distilleries. And, as Pheme had planned, we enjoyed an evening of ghost stories. And even with all those experiences, we knew there were more to be had, "We must come back!" We agreed.

In the midst of all this heart-pounding excitement, Aladar received a text from his team.

[77]

"Listen to this, Elizabeth, Aladar read, "Dr. Gallant, your team working on Angelique Forester's case has- started on the handwriting analysis. They have obtained samples from each of the suspects. As you know, though, this study of handwriting is a long, arduous process."

"Do they look for similarities, Aladar? Letter formations, curves, slants, size of letters, that kind of thing?"

"Actually, while we do look at things like that, Elizabeth, we concentrate on the differences. It's like making love"—he gave my hand a squeeze—"it's the differences that initially create the excitement. If the differences don't rule out a match, then we will look at singularities. When or if those are significant, we move from possibility to probability."

"That is so Aristotle," I said, squeezing his hand back, "'a likely impossibility is always preferable to an unconvincing possibility.'"

'Speaking of possibilities, Elizabeth," Aladar said later in the evening as if no time had passed since we last talked, and as we sipped a nightcap of the finest Scotch whiskey I ever tasted, "I haven't seen you let your hair down in quite a while. How do you feel about the possibility of letting it down tonight?"

"Literally or figuratively?" I asked, already fumbling with it in what I hoped looked like a sexy maneuver.

"Literally. I think long hair the quintessential mark of womanhood, and I think you are the quintessential woman."

[78]

"Flattery will get you everywhere," I giggled, sounding in my ears too much like a high school girl on a first date and not enough like a dignified grande dame. Nevertheless, I continued to fumble with my hair.

"Elizabeth, what is that line about hair from the fairy tale?" Aladar asked as we together reached for our drinks.

I thought for a moment and then said, "You must mean in the fairy tale *Rapunzel*."

"That's it," he said.

"'Rapunzel, Rapunzel, let down your beautiful hair,' is that the line you mean, Aladar? Whatever caused you to think of Rapunzel?"

"Your hair."

"My hair? In what context? Now? After such a busy day?"

"As I watched you all day today, I thought how sad it is that you always wear your hair up in that ballet bun."

"Sad? Why sad?"

"Because it is so beautiful when let down. I'd like to see it let down tonight. As a matter of fact, I'd like to see it let down now. Actually, I'd like to be the one to let it down. Will you let me undo it. Please?"

"You want to be my undoing?"

Aladar came over to me, stood directly in front of me, looked at me so deeply, I quivered, and said, "Elizabeth, I'm not being ambiguous here although I do think you make too much of what I say into a double entendre, like you did with the slang meaning of nob in nobbling."

[79]

"That's the fun of it, Aladar," I said reaching up to kiss him.

"I know and I do find word play exciting, but sometimes I am dead serious—like right now. Then he slowly reached for my hair, and said softly, "Elizabeth, Elizabeth, let down your beautiful hair."

Suddenly he stepped back a bit, "Why, you don't have any pins in your ballet bun! How does it stay up so nicely?"

"No pins. It's something Perla taught me. It's all in the twisting."

"Well, that's a wonderful surprise. No man wants to worry about pins."

As Aladar untwisted and loosened my hair, tenderly raking his fingers through its thickness, it cascaded down my back, and because of the manner of the twisting, it fell as if in waves.

"Oh, Elizabeth, your hair is so long! It's almost to your waist. It's so silvery, so silky, so lovely. I could lose myself in it."

Aladar gently took hold of a handful of it, whispering, "It's like a mane, a glorious mane on a glorious unicorn. You are my unicorn. You are one of a kind, dear Elizabeth. Please let me ride in your hair."

With that he put his face into the perfume of my hair while our night caps sat patiently waiting.

[80]

Chapter Nineteen

The wedding, accompanied by sequence after sequence of wedding bells, and completed with a reception that out 'Gladysed Gladys,' went beyond spectacle, beyond extravaganza, beyond memorable.

Gladys radiated unmistakable happiness. On the one hand, it was if she had waited all her life for a Dr. Henson. On the other hand, he conveyed such joy he practically burst with it, looking like a cross between a jolly old elf and a stately contented country gentleman.

After the ceremony, the bride and groom moved about the guests with alacrity and charm, greeting, hugging, kissing them, and shaking hands, patting backs. The Henson's wedding can only be described as a heightened ceremony and reception of the highest quality. One word cannot do it justice—nor can many words.

The local newspapers were abuzz with it. Their wedding even made news across the 'pond.' A New York City newspaper dubbed it, "The most glamourest (double superlative intended) wedding extravaganza ever. Gladys Kovacs, now Viscountess Gladys Henson outdid every wedding that preceded hers. No wonder she's one of the richest women in the world and one of the most admired!"

The grounds around the Inverlochy Castle provided an atmosphere not one of the classiest wedding planners could have contrived. Even the weather cooperated—low 70s and no rain! Lush green grass with white heather blooming in the distance. White heather boughs covered everything it could be festooned upon, into, or around in the foreground. Everything whispered happiness. The muted sounds of tree leaves moving in the breeze, the running river, and the waterfall intensified delightful aromas. Even the wildflowers, while soundless, added to the beauty with just the right amount of color as background—everything contributed to an absolutely gorgeous venue.

Glady arranged for tables and comfortably cushioned chairs, also decorated with heather, to be placed strategically and for easy access all over the grounds. The waitstaff, dressed in the tartan of Dr. Henson's family, a bright green plaid with stripes of light blue and darker green forming squares throughout the material, stood at attention, ready to serve.

"We must honor the Scottish foods during the wedding feast," Gladys had told us as we talked about preparations back in the States. I want the usual American foods laid out in their full splendor. No problem there as I'm flying in my personal chef from New Jersey to oversee that, but I'm trying to find the perfect chef in Scotland.

"What about Gordon Ramsay?" I suggested.

"Too much celebrity—I want someone fabulous but not quite as well known. "I'd like a woman, too, if possible."

"Then how about Susan Lawery? I know about her because she writes historical novels set in Scotland, but she's also known for promoting Scottish recipes and regional fare. She'd be wonderful."

"Do you have contact information, Lisbet? Glady asked.

"She lives in Edinburgh. Perhaps your secretary could hunt her down. She's up there in age, but so are we. I bet she'd love the challenge and you can offer her all the amenities she may need. Besides Fort William isn't that far from Edinburgh—about a three-hour drive, I think."

Glady took my suggestion and instructed her secretary to attempt to make immediate contact with Ms. Lawery.

The very next day Glady greeted me with, "We got her, Lisbet!"

"Got who?"

"Susan Lawery!"

"That's wonderful!"

"Yes. My secretary says she's perfectly delightful and is most excited about this wedding. Said she actually heard about it from someone in the burgh. Lisbet, you and I forget how quickly news spreads in small burghs. Susan and I plan to meet in a few days. In 2006, she wrote a cookbook, *A Chef Does Scotland Proud."* I intend to ask her to use it to work up that theme for our wedding—you know, prepare foods from all over Scotland."

"You still brim with ideas, Glady," I gushed not concealing my love and admiration for my older sister.

[83]

So, in addition to American fare such as all manner of hors d'oeuvres, set alongside caprese cups, an abundance of beverages, and cocktails of most anyone's choosing. Glady's personal chef produced beef and lamb kabobs, ham, bruschetta, specialty cheeses, deviled eggs, crab cakes, opulent oysters, caviar, beef with porcini mushrooms, beef sliders, mini tacos, veggie roll-ups, meatballs, grilled cheese bites, salmon, sea bass with fruit, shrimp done several ways, hand and mini meat pies, expensive monkfish, lobster, lollypop lamb chops, cheese cake tartlets, cookies, cupcakes, popsicles, Pot de Crème, macarons, macaroons, and a variety of candy.

All that sat on long tables side-by-side the choices made by Susan Lawery and her entourage: Scottish food such as trout, gannet, halibut, blue mussels, scallops, Arbroath snolies, Cullen skide chowdar, cock-a-leekie soup, Scotch pie, bannoih, haggis, shortbreads, Scottish crumpets, steak pies, black buns, grouse, sides of rumble thumps, Scottish bubble and squeak pothis, the soft drink Irn-Bru, and of course, all the varieties of Scottish whiskeys Gladys' crew could find.

Huge rotisseries were set up on the lawn. Suckling pigs and legs of mutton wound round and round wafting delicious aromas that eventually mixed with the heather and whetted appetites.

Jugglers, wending their way over the lawns, entertained the guests and delighted the children. Minstrels sang ancient Scottish romantic poetry and bagpipes rang out with traditional Scottish ballads. I felt as if I were back in the Renaissance.

[84]

Youths, holding halos of florets, rested them atop heads of girls as crowns and gifted women with bouquets of wildflowers. They placed flower buds in the *boutonnières* of the men's coats.

Fortune tellers roamed the area telling, of course, only the best and most positive futures by reading cards, hands, or small globes. "Nothing negative," instructed Glady. "This is meant to be fun not worrisome."

Jesters threaded among the guests and seemed to be everywhere. Occasionally two men would break into a mock duel, sometimes with fake swords, sometimes with play pistols.

Just when I thought things were winding down, eight riders on steeds—two black, two white, two chestnut, two dappled—captured our curiosity by riding past the castle with great flourish. After their rather triumphant first pass, a Herald, dressed in Dr. Henson's heraldry, entered the scene. He commanded our attention by playing a fanfare trumpet. Then he formally announced a joust, which he called 'a tilting'!

"Hear ye, Hear ye! A tilting will occur immediately in the adjoining *achadh,* meadow. Come ye. Come ye one and all!"

Leave it to Glady, I thought. *She apparently envisioned this tournament as the* pièce de résistance of *the entire event.*

The riders wore antique armor—*garniture complete,* that is, a complete set of armor with gauntlets, helms, mustards, pauldrons, sabatons— everything! Their weapons were reproductions of ancient weapons, as was their horses' armor, especially

[85]

the *chamfron* to protect the horses' faces. Glady had provided accurately historical costumes for everyone in the joust.

The bridal party became the traditional "Joust's Court of Honor." And as such we moved to a specially built platform above the fray.

"I don't know how I missed seeing this stadium being built," I confided to Aladar as we moved from a grassy knoll to the stadium.

"Glady can certainly camouflage things when she wants to," agreed Aladar. "I never noticed this being assembled either."

"She counted on us being busy with other things," I said mostly to assuage the guilt I felt for my own lack of observation.

Suddenly several of those fanfare trumpets blared and the Herald roared, "Let the jousts begin!" With that, Glady bestowed her ribbon upon one of the 'knights.' That rider would, in turn, return it to her on the tip of his lance after he 'won' the joust.

Speaking for us all, Pheme rhapsodized, "This is such great fun!"

Walking back after the joust to the grassy green area of the reception, we realized Bastien had been busy. There before us was a sensational wedding cake—five feet high with ten layers of sponge cake and much to my delight—macaron filling. The topper featured white heather and a gold leaf sugar sculpture that rose so high above the cake I feared it would topple—but, of course, it didn't. Just looking at it, we

[86]

all agreed that the cake was too beautiful to eat—but we ate it anyway.

"This is one time when the cake tastes as good as it looks," Loraine commented, daintily wiping a bit of frosting from her lips. "So often the cakes at weddings are beautiful works of art but have no taste."

"This is a Chris and Edwina McNulty cake," Bastien told us. "They are considered the best cake makers in Scotland.

None of us argued with that.

Chapter Twenty

We hated to leave Scotland. Much as we love our country, we all knew we would always hold Scotland as a special place in our hearts. We also knew it wouldn't take much urging on the part of Glady and Dr. Henson to convince any one of us or all of us to visit again anytime. So, we boarded "The Henson's" private jet with heavy yet happy hearts. Most of us, including the twins, slept most of the uneventful trip home.

Once home and inside our Brownstone, Aladar lost no time switching on the TV.

"Let's see what's going on in the world," he suggested.

The nightly news shocked us out of our pleasant memories. We heard the anchor say:

> Breaking News...We have just confirmed that Angelique Forester, New York City socialite and heir to the fortunes of two prestigious NYC hotels, is missing. Her home was broken into, ransacked, and plundered. Police have yet to confirm exactly what things were taken, but we do know that a valuable minaudière, a Swarkski purse in the shape of a pistol was found on her bedstand. Inside that exotic and expensive purse, investigators retrieved a handwritten note that said, 'Life isn't fair. I'm going to kill you.'
>
> The reputation of Ms. Forester in New York society, her generosity as a philanthropist, as well as the uptick in crimes in that vicinity, has caused the Police Commissioner to pledge a thorough investigation beginning immediately. More on that in our 10:00 news. In the meantime, we urge everyone in that area to be extra cautious and

[88]

careful. Please report any suspicious persons or activity immediately to this numb...."

Aladar flicked off the TV and took me in his arms. "This isn't happening," I mumbled into his jacket. "This cannot be the end to such a fairy tale wedding in our family and to all Angelique's plans."

"Then let's do something about it. Put on your trench coat, grab your magnifying glass, and abductive thinking cap, Elizabeth. We are going to find this culprit and put an end to this mystery *post haste*," declared Aladar. I never saw him more resolute.

Chapter Twenty-One

"Where are you off to so early?" I asked Aladar as he donned his coat. Suffering from jet lag, I glanced with one eye at the clock that just turned seven.

"I'm going to the office. I am determined to get to the bottom of this Angelique missing situation. After all, Elizabeth, she placed so much faith in us that night at the Chapel Bar."

"I'll do my ruminating over coffee, Aladar. But even my travel weary brain tells me we need to nail down possible motives for each of the suspects."

"Good idea. But remember: Angelique is missing, not murdered."

"True enough," I agreed.

"Then why don't you jot down reasons why or how she could be missing while you have that breakfast coffee? I'll check on whatever is going on at the precinct and then we'll put our heads together."

"Sounds like an old *Nick and Nora Charles* scene from *The Thin Man*. Shall I whip up martinis for lunch?"

"You amaze me, Elizabeth, with your breath of knowledge. Where in that magnificent brain of yours do you keep those old Nick and Nora movies?"

"I've always favored them. Now even more so as they remind me of us—sophisticated—he, the detective; she, the socialite. You know with their flirtatious bantering and excessive tippling. They even had a dog like Coco named Asta. I think he was a wire-haired terrier, though."

[90]

And with that, Aladar, leaned down to give me a kiss, "I'm not as ardent a fan of coffee as you are, Elizabeth, but it's sweet on your breath in the morning." Then out the door he went.

I fed Coco and refreshed her water, thinking all the time.

"Coco," I said aloud, "This is crazy. Why would a rich, prominent woman just disappear? How could this happen?"

Coco just looked at me as if to say, "You know why."

"You're right, Coco. I do know why. She wanted to escape. In spite of her bravado with me before I left for Scotland, she is frightened. You know what happens, don't you, Coco, when people become frightened? They downshift to their R-complex brains and react in one of the four 'F' ways: freeze, fight, flee, or engage in sexual activity—all meant as escape."

Coco laid down and closed her eyes, apparently unaware of the 4Fs. I was not to be deterred. Taking another slip of coffee, I told Coco my theory.

"Coco, I think Angelique chose to flee. And I think I know where she fled—to her winter cabin in the Poconos."

Coco opened her eyes and agreed with a wide yawn.

"Oh, sure easy for you to be bored with my conclusion, but you'll be yawning another yawn if I'm correct." And with that I chucked Coco under her chin. Then I picked up my iPhone and sent a brief text to Angelique.

[91]

Hi Angelique!
Elizabeth here. Back from Scotland.
I need to talk to you. Please call me ASAP.

Just as I hoped, within the hour, Angelique called.

"When did you get back? Was it wonderful? The society columns are replete with 'The Wedding of the Century.' What have you heard about my case? What have you found out, Elizabeth? I didn't want to burden you before your sister's wedding and all the festivities and yack and yammer, but I'm worried to death. And with my other minaudière missing!"

"Never mind the missing minaudière. Right now, Angelique—you're missing! Haven't you heard the news?"

"I want to be missing, Elizabeth. I think that will throw the culprit off guard."

"That's an interesting theory. Have you received any more notes?"

"Yes. This last one held a drawing of an eye. That was all. After I found it, I left town."

"Did you report it?"

"No, I knew you were due back soon, so I thought I'd wait and fill you in on all the details when you returned. When can you and Aladar come up here?"

"I think we better come as soon as he can get away."

"Great. Text me."

"See, Coco, I was right all along. Angelique orchestrated her own escape. Now who's yawning?"

[92]

Chapter Twenty-Two

"Aladar, I spoke to Angelique today."

"What? You did? She's missing and you talked to her? How did that happen? Where is she?"

"She's in her winter home in the Poconos. How it happened is not important right now, but what is important is that she wants us to come up there. She has a beautifully appointed place in those mountains. I've been there once. I think we should go, leave immediately. If we take Highway 80, we can be there in about two hours. And the weather is conducive."

"I agree. Let's go. You can fill me in on the details on the way."

Already in slacks and a sweater, I grabbed my puffy coat, pulled on my Lous Vuitton desert boots that were far too chic for a quick visit in the mountains, but with a two-inch clunky heel they would do if walking was involved. I jammed my Prada wool bucket hat on my head and announced, "I'm ready."

"Well, don't you look cute as button," Aladar enthused, stopping to check me out even before he opened the door. "You look like an advertisement for *Outdoor Girl*—not like a sleuth on a mission."

"More like *Outdoor Elderly Woman*," I corrected, even though I secretly loved being called a girl. "Never know when the paparazzi will sprout up," I joked.

For a minute I thought our joy with wordplay and allusion would overshadow the importance of this trip, but Aladar bolted out the door and quickly started his car, which luckily was parked out front. Following him, I jumped in. Off we went.

"She's frightened, Aladar, very frightened." I continued my comments. "She didn't want to worry us before the wedding, but she wants our help now."

"Did she offer any additional information?"

"Not yet, but she definitely wants to talk to us."

"Well, we're on our way." And with that, Aladar gunned the motor. His marvelous machine made a little jump that reminded me of Coco when she's excited.

As we wound upwards around the Poconos to our destination, we couldn't help but notice the leaves—all brilliant yellows, golds, browns, various shades green. We remarked on the beauty of that yearly phenomenon several times during the drive. Autumn was in the air. We could sense it even before inhaling that woodsy-ness we associated with the season—part pine trees, part maple leaves, part pumpkins, part spices, part apples, part wood burning fires, part wonderful love—part—not-so-wonderful death.

Death.

Then, like some invisible ghost, autumn began to permeate our thoughts, even our bones. Not my favorite time of the year—too much dying—flowers drying up, plants withering, grasses turning brown.

This season is oxymoronic, I thought. *To be sure leaves turn lively colors, but then they lifelessly fall off the branches. Those leafless sticks remind me of skeleton bones. Animals burrow away to hide, to hibernate—everything prepares for death. Persephone accompanies Hades into the Underworld. This is such a dreary time.*

[94]

I shook my head. These thoughts coming unbidden depressed me, stood over me like some specter of ill will. Slowly an ominous feeling enveloped me as if the specter wanted to invade my being, carry me off. I hoped it wasn't a premotion.

I shook my head again to rid this feeling that was beginning to overpower me. I almost wanted Aladar to turn around and head back home. "Aladar...," I began.

"Did Angelique seem in good spirits?" Aladar asked simultaneously. His voice, holding the challenge of a new case within it, whisked away my forbidding feelings. I told myself, *everything is going to be all right.* I stayed positive for the remainder of the drive.

Chapter Twenty-Three

We slid into Angelique's driveway in just under two hours. "Thank heavens for GPS and no traffic," Aladar said as if reading my thoughts about remaining positive.

"We made good time," I agreed.

Angelique opened the door before we rang the bell. Clearly, she had been waiting and watching for us. She looked a bit disheveled but greeted us with her usual aplomb. "Come in, come in. Oh, Darling, that's a charming bucket hat. How are you doing these days, Aladar? How was Scotland?"

We shook the cold from our coats and the chill from our minds, and settled into what Angelique called her winter hide-a-way. Ironically, as events unfurled, we discovered her place wasn't hidden enough.

With a low fire smoldering in her massive fireplace fashioned from natural stone created by minerals cooling and compressing millions of years ago and being recently excavated from a local quarry to create this hearth, Aladar began.

"How are you doing, Angelique?" Aladar asked as she served us drinks.

"As good as can be expected, I guess. I want this to be over. I hate to be a coward, but soon after you left for Scotland, I found a strange note under my door."

"What did it say?" Aladar and I asked in unison.

"Nothing. That's the eerie part of it. All it had was an eye drawn on it, which I recognized immediately

[96]

as 'The Eye of Horus.' The eye itself was colored green—with a crayon, I think."

"Do you still have it?" Aladar asked.

"Yes, yes, of course, right here. I knew you'd want to see it."

Angelique reached into a small drawer in the table next to the coffee-colored leather sofa and took out a manilla folder from which she extracted the drawing. It looked to be standard 9" X 12" drawing paper, the kind available most anywhere. I instinctively knew that paper wouldn't lead anywhere but hoped the drawing might. We both leaned into it, examining it as best we could without any equipment.

"I'll need to take this in..." Aladar began. Angelique interrupted him "... I knew you'd want it. That's why I put it in the folder."

"Someone just slipped it under your door?" I asked again to give us breathing time.

And in that moment, I began to get that lightheaded feeling, that thrumming in my head like a rotating propeller, ending with what I always called clarity of thought. When that dizzy feeling left me, I usually had a renewed insight or a deeper or a different way of looking at things. Sometimes it was a totally different way of thinking. Always helpful, I hoped it would bring me some new insights now. Time seemed crucial.

"Yes. What do you think it means? Darling, you are good at inferring," Angelique pressed. "Do you think it's someone who lives in my high rise? If so, why would they want to kill me?"

"Well, one thing seems obvious. Coloring the eye green almost admits to jealousy."

"But don't you think that's too cliché, especially since I actually have green eyes? And those of us with green eyes are in such a small minority?"

"I don't know, but I find myself asking, why only one eye? And why no words, no written message? I'm baffled," I admitted.

"I thought maybe the culprit just wants this note to scare me. But it didn't."

"It didn't?"

"No, it just struck me as odd because it matches a tattoo I have—one I had done for protection. I thought maybe that made it a good sign."

"You have a tattoo? I never noticed it. Where is it hiding?" I asked, taken totally off guard by this new information, thinking *it may be on her breast or her bottom.*

"Here."

Angelique turned her left arm so that we could see the fleshy part between her elbow and shoulder joint. Her tattoo was in the axilla, the armpit, the area directly under the shoulder joint.

"Why, Angelique, this drawing exactly matches your tattoo, even down to the eye color. When you raise your arm, the eye opens wide as if it's staring straight ahead, opening the world to your tattoo," I observed, stating what Angelique already knew and Aladar could see for himself.

"I think you are right about it not scaring you— not with such a match—but how did that match happen? It can't be coincidental. Who knew about your tat and whatever possessed you to get such a tattoo in the first place?" Aladar asked.

Angelique just stared at us for a moment. I felt her eyes and that freaky tattoo's eye on me. I thought of Hanaka's eyes. I rubbed my own. I realized Angelique was deliberating about what to tell us. After a pause, she said, "When I was in grad school I got involved with an Egyptologist."

"You never mentioned that," I accused.

"I thought he was so handsome with his darker skin, jet black hair, prominent nose, broad shoulders and tapered waist. He was perfect looking, but his ways were different from mine. Much he did as ritual. Everything had meaning to him. You would have loved him, Darling, appreciating words and symbols as you do."

"Give us an example," I suggested.

"Well, he wore an amulet all the time. When I asked him about it, he told me it continued the image of what he called 'a protective deity.' This same deity also turned up in his apartment on a tiny corner shelf. He would put flowers in front of it. 'These flowers keep me in the good graces of that god and help me ward off evil.' He replaced those flowers weekly. They were symbolic to him."

"Sounds quaint," remarked Aladar.

"In a real way, he was quaint, but he had other qualities. As fascinating as he was sexy, he taught me many things, especially about Egyptology, more specifically about the Eye of Ra and the Eye of Horus. He explained that Ra represents power whereas Horus represents protection and health. He insisted I get a tat

[99]

of Horus. 'It will protect you the way my amulet protects me,' he told me."

"Odd it shows up now," I murmured.

"As you know, Darling, I was conservative and somewhat afraid of what my father would say about such a thing. Tattoos were not the rage they are now, so I chose a place on my body that was obscure, a place my father wouldn't likely look."

"Obscure is right," I said, "I never noticed it." *First, I don't notice the stadium being built in Scotland and now I never noticed this tat. Some sleuth I am,* I thought chiding myself to be more observant.

"Another thing, Ra is the sun; Horus is the moon. The eyes are identical in appearance except Horus is the left eye and Ra the right eye. Can you tell which one I have?" Angelique challenged.

Again, Aladar and I examined Angelique's arm.

"Looks like the left eye to me. What do you think, Elizabeth?"

"I agree."

"You're correct. At the time I wanted Horus' protection and his promise of good health—still do for that matter. Which one do you think was drawn on the note I received?"

Again we examined the drawing, looking closely. We decided the sketch matched Angelique's tattoo exactly. Both sketch and tat duplicated the Eye of Horus—the left eye.

Unable to tamp down my curiosity, I asked, "Whatever happened to this Egyptologist? To him and you?"

"Life. Reality. My father almost went berserk when he met him and found out we were serious. He was too different; my father had no place to put him in his tightly held schemata of life."

Aladar cleared his throat and brought us back to the present—intentionally, I'm sure, "I think there's more to this eye business. Let's brainstorm some things we associate with eyes, eyes as symbols, anything eyes."

"That's a great idea, Aladar," I said.

He asked, "Elizabeth, will you be our scribe?"

"Of course."

Angelique was about to get me paper, but I pointed to my laptop.

"Oh sure," she said lightly tapping her forehead with the palm of her hand. "Dah," she said.

"The way this works is we say anything associated with eyes that pops into our heads—me too—and we can also piggyback on what each other offers! Ideas generate ideas. Ready, set, go," Aladar said as if he were hosting a game show.

We began calling out words: "seeing, sight, blindness, big, shifty, squinty," I typed in the words as fast as I could, abbreviating some to keep up, "have a wandering eye, light, darkness, God sees all things, omniscience, Eye of Ra, Horus, protection, life, lunar trait, third eye, spiritual eye, intuitive eye, eye for an eye, apple of my eye, perception, direction, new direction, prophecy, fortune telling, smart, awareness, intelligence, open your eyes, close your eyes, vision, optometrist, ophthalmologist, pupil, retina, enlightenment, knowledge, eye drops, wisdom, myopia, eagle eye, a sight for sore eyes, snake eyes, keep your

[101]

eye peeled, turn a blind eye, cry your eyes out, a black eye, green eyes, baby blues."

"Stop! Time's up," Aladar called out.

"Good. I couldn't think of anything more," I confessed.

Aladar said, "Elizabeth, can you print those words?"

"Sure."

Looking over what I printed, Aladar said, "We have quite a list here. I want us to read over this list several times and then circle the word or words that strike us as possibly being most closely associated with the drawing Angelique found under her door or the one on her arm. We might jot down our reasons, too, or even other connections. Then we'll share and see if this step triggers anything further."

This was beginning to feel more like a college psych class on free association or a parlor game than an investigation, but we all willingly participated. Besides offering hope, it was fun!

Chapter Twenty-Four

At some point in our circling of words and making notes, Angelique asked, "Anyone hungry?"

I was famished and suspected Aladar was, too. We hadn't eaten anything since early morning, but we both barely nodded to be polite.

"I bet you are. You're both too genteel to admit it. Let me scrounge around the kitchen and get us something," Angelique said.

"Please don't fuss. Do you want some help?" I asked.

"I'd love some," she said almost too quickly. I realized while her offer of food was sincere, it also provided a ruse to get me alone. *What does Angelique have on her mind?* I thought.

I must admit, while not as opulent as her New York City place, this 'cabin'—as she called it—was a misnomer if I ever saw one. It held a delightful postwar knotty pine kitchen. Simple yet rustic, its old-timey appearance belied all the modern conveniences tucked within it.

As we gathered some cold chicken and appropriate accoutrements from the fridge, pantry, and cabinets, Angelique whispered, "I'm glad to have you alone."

"Why?"

"I feel silly about this in front of so esteemed an investigator—with his doctorate no less—and your friend."

"Don't feel that way, Angelique, Aladar is quite down-to-earth and most eager to solve this situation."

"Is it too arrogant of me to find it hard to believe someone really wants to kill me?"

"Not at all. People are strange creatures with all kinds of motives, motives that evolve because of curious circumstances. You are a student of literature, Angelique, you have read all the intricacies of jealousy. You know its power. This entire matter seems to me unquestionably rooted in jealousy—down to the green eye. What about your Egyptologist?"

"Oh, he's long gone from the scene." She dismissed him so quickly, I believed her. "But why would anyone be jealous of me? I try to be generous. I try to be philanthropic. I'm not a greedy person," she pleaded for understanding, those beautiful green eyes tearing up.

"I know that about you, Angelique, but apparently the culprit holds deeply entrenched notions, convoluted ones, obviously incorrect ones—most probably motives not even directly caused by anything you did or did not do."

"There's something else..."

"What is that, Angelique? *What is it about Angelique that she holds back some things?* I asked myself.

"I saw the intruder."

"You what? You did? That's valuable information! What did the intruder look like?"

"That's just it. I didn't actually see much. That's why I didn't want to embarrass myself in front of your friend."

[104]

"Then tell me what you did see."

"I short skinny person in a black body suit—vest style—like scuba divers wear but without the feet."

"That's it?"

"Yes, because this person snuck up behind me, grabbed me, lifted my left arm, and bit me right on that Eye of Horus tattoo and then ran off. It all happened so fast; I was both frightened and surprised. I only caught a glimpse of a skinny body clad in black. Like a fool, I just stood there."

"That strikes me as a normal reaction—part of those 4Fs. You froze," I said to comfort her.

"It's as if the intruder wanted to bite that tat off, get rid of it. If I didn't know better, I'd think my father had sent someone from his grave to do the deed—rid me of the tattoo he hated. See now why I didn't want Aladar to hear that? Even in the retelling, it sounds preposterous."

"Really, Angelique?"

"Really, Darling!"

"Okay then. Let me think about this. The intruder must have known you, known about that tat under your arm. His or her actions were too deliberative to be just by chance. Seems like the Egyptologist wouldn't want to eliminate what he recommended," I said, already ruling him out as a suspect.

"Besides, Akmun would never do such a thing."

"Let's munch now and let all this settle as we see what Aladar has determined." I steered Angelque back to her seat in front of the fireplace. *But 'motive' kept ringing in my mind. Motive. We must find the motive.*

That will give us some answers. Come on clarity of thought, I silently begged.

By this time, the fire had burned down, so Aladar put a few more logs on. As the flames grew, as if alive, I felt my understanding of the eye symbolism becoming clearer. I eagerly awaited our collective analysis. I felt comfortable in my element.

"Our responses varied," Aladar began. "Angelique circled *blindness, God sees all things,* and *omniscience.* Elizabeth circled *open your eyes, keep your eyes peeled, awareness, snake eyes,* and *the eye of RA.* I circled *protection, knowledge,* and *myopia.*"

"I suggest we apply abductive reasoning to these results," I said.

"Good. Let's do that."

"What's abductive reasoning?" Angelique asked plainly forgetting the lectures in logic from our university years. Just as obviously she was not nearly as smitten with C.S. Peirce, the theoretician who proposed abduction as a way of thinking as I continue to be. *How could she have forgotten him when he made such an impression on me? I asked myself. Well, we were in different places,* I reasoned her excuse.

Aladar turned to me and gestured for me to go ahead with the explanation before we proceeded.

"In a nutshell, abductive reasoning concentrates on noting the easiest or best explanation of the situation. The simplest explanation is usually the preferred one. Scholars have determined that the simplest explanation is most often the true and valid explanation of the situation, in this case, of a crime."

"Is that like telling people taking a test if they are conflicted by two or more choices to go with their instinct, their first choice? Statistically, that's usually the right answer?

"Could be like that, Angelique, although I've read that lately that theory is questionable."

"Whatever," I continued, "taking that explanation, the sleuth goes on to use deduction and induction or both to reason that simple explanation through to its logical conclusion. In that way, hypotheses—not instinctual responses—can sometimes be proven."

"Got it. Let's do it." Angelique was ready.

"Well, if we merge all our circles in our search for the simplest," Aladar said, "we come up with something like: The answer is known by God or RA or Horus and those who open their eyes. Or conversely, if you are blind or myopic, you will not see the answer. You will not gain the knowledge."

"So, if we just open our eyes, we will find the culprit."

"Exactly. Peirce would say, look for the easiest, most glaring solution. What are we looking at and not seeing?"

Aladar offered, "The culprit by way of the motive of the culprit. We need to become omniscient. We need to look at each suspect with the eye of the gods, so to speak, ferret out the motive. That means we need in-depth interviews with each suspect. And we need our listening ears and all-seeing eyes working overtime during those interviews."

Chapter Twenty-Five

"That was productive," I said somewhat satisfied as we rode home, the massage on the passenger side of Aladar's Mercedes relaxing my back, neck, and mind. "But did you notice the bite mark around that tattoo?"

"No, I can't say that I did until she told us about it."

"Me either. That tattoo and those marks are in an inconspicuous place. I'm no forensic scientist, but just from that quick look, I'd say they were human not animal teeth marks. She was also a bit bruised."

"The intruder, no doubt. I'll get right on this case tomorrow, but tonight, Elizabeth, let's let all this information percolate."

I jumped at the chance for word play. "Percolate as in make coffee? Or Percolate as to trickle? Or percolate as to become lively? Or percolate as to penetrate?" I emphasized the last meaning.

The car swerved.

"Elizabeth, you are going to cause me to drive right off this winding road with your word antics."

"Oh, bosh! Surely, you can handle some playful bantering."

"Sometimes I think you underestimate your power over me."

Chapter Twenty-Six

Aladar didn't waste any time. The next morning, he began contacting the suspects. The doorman, the domestic, and the woman who collected the soils, whom we had never seen, were first on the list. We six former college classmates dribbled along last on the list.

"I'll decide about the cabinet installers and constructions workers after the first round of Q & A, if interviewing them seems necessary," Aladar said. Truthfully, he didn't think they fit into the Isabelle Fayette culture—too unlettered to know the value or history of her work or that of Fabergé—so he reasoned, at least at first, that they probably wouldn't be interested in robbing or threatening Angelique.

When he told me that, I told him those pieces might appeal to any man as possible gifts. He countered with their impossibly high prices. We left it at that. Even so, Aladar kept their contact information handy, putting possible interviews with those people on hold.

"We'll be conducting the interviews in here," Aladar said, gesturing me toward that tiny room at the precinct. *Why do I keep having to come to this claustrophobic place? Oh, well, Elizabeth,* I said to myself, *you better get used to it. You have at least nine or ten people to observe being interviewed.*

A forensic interrogator sat behind a plain oak table with a sheaf of papers in front of him. He never referred to them overtly that I could see, asking his questions with an impressive depth of memory.

Aladar and I sat in the back of the room. After a short time, he leaned over and whispered, "I have another appointment. Take good notes. See you back home." And he blew me a kiss. I puckered one back.

Working with Aladar's team and the NYC Police Department's Investigative Unit, suspects were gathered as if in some Agatha Christie novel. The doorman was their top suspect but not mine. Angelique's domestic, Mary, seemed their second choice, but my first choice, after all, she worked for Angelique every day. I knew the kind of bond Perla and I had forged over the years, so perhaps Angelique and Mary had some sort of bond as well—one that may have erupted or corrupted over time.

They also called in this woman who collected the soils. Finally, they called the six of us who had participated in our sixty-fifth college pre-reunion at Angelique's. Least likely Angelique—Hanaka, Cathy, Umbuya, Franny—and extremely unlikely, me.

At that moment the doorman lumbered into the room. A large beefy man, who walked and held himself erect in the manner of a proper doorman at a proper establishment, which gave him a bit of class and made him look taller; yet, in an odd way, he seemed more approachable.

"Please state your name, age, occupation." The Q & A had begun.

"My name is Alfred Muska. I am fifty-eight years old, and I work as a doorman for 432 Park Avenue."

[110]

"Have you even been in the residence of 'One double A' in that building?"

"Yes, that is where Ms. Angelique Forester lives. She sometimes calls me to do errands for her."

"So, you're familiar with its layout."

"Yes, Sir. But only the front rooms, Sir."

He was asked to describe them, which he did in great detail. I tried not to overtly wince at his grammar. He obviously omitted any reference to the bedrooms.

"Were you aware of Ms. Forester's collections?"

"Not really, Sir."

"Did Ms. Forester ever show you any of her collections?"

"No, Sir."

"What kinds of errands did you do for her?"

"Mostly I was picking up something from department stores or taking something over to one of her friends. Sometimes she was wanting me to get her something fast food—Chinese mostly."

"Do you have any idea where she might be now?"

"Maybe her place in the Poconos."

"How do you know she has a place in the Poconos?"

"She was telling me about it one time."

"How did that conversation happen?"

"She was waiting for me to call her a cab. She and me was making small talk."

"Do you know its address?"

"No sir. I only know it's in those mountains."

"Can you think of any reason why she might be missing?"

"No sir."

"Nothing unusual?"

"Only there was this here man who come once a while back and said he was her father."

"Why was that unusual—a father visiting his daughter?"

"Because he wasn't the same guy Ms. Forester introduced me to once as her father. I remember faces. It helps when you're a doorman."

"Interesting. What did this man do or say to you?"

"He was wanting her residence number. I told him he needed to ask the receptionist. Said he was her father. I still wouldn't give him her number. I was wondering why he didn't have her number. I mean him being her father and all. Then he goes into the building."

"Was he in there long?"

"I don't know. I got busy and have to stay alert to comings and goings beings if I want to keep my job. But all visitors have to show IDs. You could ask the receptionist."

"What did this alleged father look like?"

"He stood taller than me. Dark hair with some grey. Lots of hair for an older guy. I noticed beings I'm losing mine. Big black mustache—the bushy kind, but neat. He give me a big tip, he did."

"What did he do when he came out?"

"He was wanting me to hail him a cab."

"Did he give you an address?"

"No, he must a gave it directly to the cabbie once he was inside the taxi."

"Anything unusual after that?"

[112]

"Only that Ms. Forester comes out right after he goes."

"Do you think he saw her coming out?"

"No."

"Do you think she saw him?"

"No. They was missing each other."

"What did she do?"

"She was wanting me to call her cab."

"Where did she go?"

"Now that I think about it—that there were the odd thing. "

"What was odd about it?"

"She was wanting to go to the Surrogate's Courthouse."

"Isn't that where historical records such as birth, deaths, and marriages for the five boroughs are housed?"

"Yes Sir. That's what I think. Never been there myself."

Sitting there, hearing that, I remembered that the Surrogate's Courthouse is sometimes called the Municipal Archives. I had some business there a couple of times. It's only about ten minutes or so from Park Avenue. *Why would Angelique rush there immediately after this John Doe aka 'father' visited her? Who is this John Doe with the big black mustache?"* I asked myself. I had no answer, so I decided to visit the Surrogate's Courthouse in the near future myself.

Chapter Twenty-Seven

The interview with the woman who collects the soils was brief. She stated her name as Jane Schnake. A short skittish anorexic looking woman, she either didn't know anything or she was keeping what she did know to herself. She reiterated her story of slipping in and out of Angelique's home and the homes of others in that high-rise building solely to gather the soils and replace them. It was her job, she said, to be invisible. "I get paid to be transparent," were her very words. No amount of clever or circuitous questioning, probing, or prodding elicited anything further. She adamantly repeated, "I have no idea where Ms. Forester is." *She's a smart one,* I thought.

Mary Astor, the domestic, was another matter. She was chubby and pleasant looking, except for the pock marks that covered her face. She had a funny arm, which she tried unsuccessfully to hide with wide sleeves. Gabby and forthcoming, she offered many unsolicited details, asides, opinions, and conclusions. I thought, *a jury will love her; a lawyer for the plaintiff will love her, the lawyer for the defendant—maybe not so much.*

What did bring a gasp from the attendees in that tiny room was Ms. Astor's answer to the question: "How did you happen to work for Angelique Forester?"

"She's my sister. I know it, but she doesn't or at least she didn't." That answer demanded further questions with hopefully revealing answers. That fact was not lost on the interrogator. Nor on Angelique, who just shook her head. *I bet over the years Angelique has had many people claiming kinship.*

"And just how do you know that?"

"Ma told me when I was little. At first, she told me Angelique was my half-sister, that we had different Pa's, but later she admitted that me and Angelique had the same Pa."

"Can you tell us exactly what your mother told you?"

"Sure can. She told me this years ago, but I remember like it was yesterday. I have one of those 'photogenic' memories. Said she was a kid when she met Pa. Said he was handsome and rich and she was young and pretty. Said he swept her off her feet, bought her nice things, expensive things, and took her to nice places. Then he just took her."

"Took her?"

"You know. He did it with her."

"Did it?"

"You know, they had sex. Then she got preggy with me. He didn't want me first off, and after I was born, he especially didn't want me when he saw my withered arm."

"You were born with a withered arm?" The chief interrogator asked to clarify. I'm sure he wanted to make certain the arm was withered at birth and not damaged in an accident of some sort. I'm sure he was thinking ahead.

"Ma said I was a 'blue baby.' Said I was born with my arm around my head. Said that did something to the oxygen. Said that made my arm weak and withered. I still can work good, though. Ask anybody. I'm a good

[115]

worker. Said once Pa saw it, he didn't want to have nothin' to do with me or Ma either after that. Said, 'I don't want a deformed kid with a funny arm. There's nothin' wrong with me or anyone in my family. This freak musta come from you.' Ma told me he called me a freak. I wish she never told me that."

"How did that make you feel?"

"It hurt me bad. I cried my eyes out."

"So, Ma didn't want to have nothin' to do with him neither—you know, it was a pride thing. We was poor but we had our pride. He made her swear not to tell nobody about him or me. Said he'd kill her if she did and he found out. Ma believed him. He scared her. He scared me, too—that big mustache that moved up and down when he talked scared me. I had nightmares about it."

"Did you tell your mother about those nightmares."

"I sure did. She cried, too."

"Then what happened?"

"Come to find out he already had a girlfriend, a rich girlfriend. But then maybe he found religion or read something because one day he calls Ma and tells her he heard of some cure for me. Said I had Erb's Palsey, and they could put me in a machine and stretch my arm to make it right. But the hospital needed to see proof I was his kid.

"They got married again to get the certificate, and then Ma had Angelique—Angelique Astor— 'their little angel.' I must admit, she was beautiful, not ugly like me. She was perfect with red ringlets of curls all over her head and green eyes, not like me with these

[116]

scars on my face, my crappy hair, and withered arm. Ma said the newspapers was all over them. Said she read all about herself—Rosa Bloomfield—that was her name first off and my father—Kensington Astor. Him from the rich Astor's and their beautiful angel—Angelique—read most every day about him and her in the newspapers. There was lots of pictures of them, too. Nobody took my picture. Nobody said anything about me in them newspapers."

"Why do you think that was the case? Mary?"

"I was their loser. I went with Ma to some place with big machines and such, but it all came crashing down when my arm didn't get any better and some newspaper guy got wind of it. He come to the hospital. I told him how it hurt so bad when they put me in that stretcher contraption."

"Sounds terrible."

"Someone at the newspaper said it was like a medieval torture machine. Wrote a big, long article in the *New York Gazette* about my deformity and what they was doing to me. Called it Brachial Plexus and made it sound awful, maybe more awful than it was, but it was and still is awful."

"Did your father go with you?"

"My father he was big in society. He couldn't take it or didn't want all that bad stuff. Him and Ma split. Ma tried to push him against the wall for money, but then he claimed he didn't know her. Turned the tables on her and told the law my Ma was harassing him, making things up to ruin his reputation, to leech money. It got real nasty. Ma finally just gave up."

"How much of this story does Angelique know?"

[117]

"She doesn't know none of it, I don't think—too little to remember—she was like one-year old or littler and Ma didn't tell her, me neither. Didn't even tell me 'til later. I never said a word to Angelique. Plus, my father ignored me."

"Did that hurt you?"

"More than the machines. For Angelique, he hired nannies, even sent her to an expensive pre-school for babies, but within that year he left me, too. He took Angelique away from Ma. Got a court order. Ma tried to raise a ruckus, but he threatened her more and with horrible stuff, so she raised me herself. Ma got me; Pa got Angelique. Those were different times. End of story."

"Is it really the end, Ms. Astor?" The Interrogator asked. *Now's that's hitting hard,* I thought.

"Hell no! I'm jealous as all hell get out of my sister. She got it all and still gets everything! Pa's an old, old man now, but he still goes to see her in that big car with a driver. Sometimes he sends his 'man,' calls his valet 'his man,' to take her money, I guess. His man sometimes claims he's Angelique's father. Me and Ma got—get nothing. We worked our tails off for everything. And now Ma's gone— I guess Pa's gone, too."

"So, how did that ultimately affect you?" *This feels like a heavy bag workout with Marythe punching bag.*

"I made a plan in my head to work for my sister so's I could get close to her. Maybe after a time, we could be like sisters should. Then I got the idea to kidnap her. I wasn't gonna hurt her, mind you, just scare

[118]

her good. Maybe get some money. Maybe talk to her. Ransom, you know. Make it easier for me. Give me some satisfaction, I don't know—you know."

"Did you kidnap Angelique Forester?" *The knock-out punch?*

"No. I just was wanting to. But I guess I'm too chicken. I'm like my Ma."

Chapter Twenty-Eight

"I love it, Aladar, I love that we have Perla who always makes certain we have sustenance. Look what I found in the fridge—diced tomatoes, shredded lettuce, grated cheese, chopped onions, cooked black beans, and bags of tortilla chips—the big ones and the little ones—all that on hand if we get the 'munchies.' Tonight she even browned and seasoned some hamburger meat and left it for us to warm up."

"Sounds like a nacho night to me," Aladar said. "*Bendiciones*, Perla," he said almost like a prayer, digging into the ingredients with gusto, divvying them on top of the tortillas and tortilla chips mumbling, "*Tengo hambre.*"

That preparation out of the way, and a platter of nachos within arm's reach, he said with his mouth full of nachos, "Fill me in on what I missed of the Q & A today. I'll make us a couple of margaritas. Good with you?"

With my own mouthfull of nachos, I nodded, choosing one particularly loaded chip, I held it aloft, took a bite, swallowed, and began a retelling of the day's drilling. I concluded my summation with, "What do you think we learned today?"

After a reflective pause, and a sip of Margarita, Aladar said, "We learned that everyone is jealous in one way or another of Angelique?"

"Do you think things happen to us serendipitously or do you think we bring things on ourselves?"

"What, Elizabeth, brought about so erudite a question?"

"When I sat in on Mary Astor's Q & A, Angelique's domestic and alleged sister, I got to thinking."

"Dangerous."

"Oh, do be serious, Aladar."

"Mary claims her mother marries and has her by a rich prominent fellow when they were young. He ultimately rejects them both. But then she remarries him, after he appears to come to his senses. But he really doesn't—leopards don't change their spots. Second time around, she has Angelique," I said.

"Sounds like bad decision-making," Aladar commented.

"I agree. Those situations were brought about, in my opinion, by bad decisions, or rather one bad decision made twice. In my mind, Mary's mother brought on their own problems."

"Bad for Mary not so bad for Angelique," Aladar pointed out.

"But the Q & A of Hanaka that followed Mary struck me as a totally different scenario."

"In what way?"

"Hanaka seems to have been affected by fate, by the stars, by destiny, bad luck, kismet, by divine will, or some such inevitability in a different way."

"I sense a story coming," Aladar said.

"If I didn't know you better, I'd think you were intentionally bedeviling me."

"Now why would I want to do that?"

"Because I have already bewitched you! And now you want to bewitch me."

"Hush, Elizabeth," Aladar whispered conspiratorially, his hand making a parenthesis around the corner of his mouth, although no one was about. "We don't want anyone knowing about our word play, thinking it's more than a game."

"Right. Think on this then, Aladar. Hanaka comes from money and status—old money and ancient status—from a venerable culture going back thousands of years."

"How does that factor in?"

"I remember one day at the university when several of us girls were unpacking after Christmas vacation, Hanaka unpacked the most beautiful kimono I had ever seen. It was pure white made of the finest silk with intricate braiding and some sort of gold designs that looked like miniature crowns throughout the material. 'Do model it,' we begged her. 'We want to see you wearing it.'

"In her fastidious way, Hanaka put her jika-tabi on her feet and then slipped her kimono over what she had on. She wound the heavily brocaded Obi that came in the box with the kimono carefully around her waist. She looked like a Japanese princess, a Hime. All she needed was a flower in her hair."

"What are those designs?" asked Cathy, our impetuous one.

"Those are the signs of our family," she explained always so humble. Then she added,

"They are like our family crest."

[122]

"That's when we knew our classmate, Hanaka Haruki, was a descendent of a Japanese dynasty. And that's when we knew she had many obligations and lived with many more complicated structures than we did."

"What's that got to do with Mary Astor?"

"Once grown and out from under the thumb of a rather authoritarian father and a strict culture, once here in America, Hanaka made her own decision to have a blepharoplasty—you know that surgery that gives the eyelid a crease."

"I've heard of it."

"She underwent that surgery with a noted surgeon in the field—but careful as she had been in choosing her surgeon and careful as that noted surgeon was—here's where Fate stepped in—either the knife or the hand slipped damaging her left eye. Well, she reasoned after the initial shock, she could make do with one eye, but then because her doctors were working with and studying her eyes, they discovered retinitis pigmentosa, or R.P., a rare disease."

"How terrible."

"Cathy told me that Hanaka told her, 'As the disease progresses, the rod cells around the edges of my retina will die, then the cones will die. My vision will contract, so it will be like looking through a paper-towel roll that becomes smaller and smaller. Before long, my vison will permanently contract; I'll be completely blind.'"

"When questioned further, Hanaka admitted that while she admired and liked Angelique, she resented her. When I listened to her answer the

[123]

jealousy question, I understood and felt so sorry for her."

"How *did* she answer that question?"

She said, "Angelique has her eyes, what more can I say? She can see; I cannot. What more can I say?"

"Then she was asked, "Did you mean to do Angelique harm, Hanaka?" She admitted, "I was insanely jealous of her. I spent every hour of every day thinking of her good fortune and my bad fortune, but I could never harm her."

"I believed her. What do you think, Aladar, do things happen to us because of our decisions or because of the alignment of planets?"

Chapter Twenty-Nine

"What about this Cathy Melather? Aladar asked. What did Q & A reveal about her?"

"Cathy never had money like most of us. She was one of the few girls at that time on a work scholarship at the university. I remember her waiting on our table."

"Your classmates waited on tables?" Aladar asked, seemingly incredulous.

"Yes. Strange now but then some of those girls on work scholarships waited on the rest of us. Those not on work scholarships sat at tables of about six or eight for our meals and were waited on by the scholarship girls. Cathy was a scholarship girl."

"Amazing. Didn't that fester discontent?"

I chose to ignore the question, surprised Aladar asked it.

"These tables were always fully set appropriately for breakfast, lunch, and dinner. Each place was complete with the silverware placed one inch from the edge of the table, utensils placed in the order of use—outside in. While we learned forks go to the left of the plate whereas knives and spoons go to the right of it, I always remembered the order a different way, a way taught to me as a child."

"How was that, Elizabeth?"

"The mommy is the fork. All the other mommies (or the children, depending on the version) walk by her side or on the sidewalk (napkin)to the left of the house (plate). The daddy is the knife. All the other daddies (utensils) walk with him to the right of the house (plate). The butter knife, placed across its own plate, goes above the mommy; the glasses—water, wine or whatever—go above the daddy. If there's a dessert fork or spoon, they go above the house (plate). Simple. Easy to remember."

"Cute idea for kids."

"I still sometimes think 'mommy and daddy' as I set the table," I confessed, smiling at the remembrance.

"At the university, there was China, crystal, silver, and a crisp white tablecloth, fresh each day, covering the table. We even had napkin rings—most of us had our own engraved with our initials to personalize them. Using those rings, we kept our own napkins for one week's use separated from the napkins of others."

"That was exceedingly sanitary," Aladar laughed.

"And we were served as if we were in a restaurant. All that never overwhelmed me. I took it for granted. We were being readied for a world of correct etiquette and polish, although I already knew most of it. I guess I thought everyone knew it, too."

"Your mother taught you well."

"She did. But for good measure, the nuns walked around the tables as we ate and checked our manners. If one of us forgot and put an elbow on the table, the nun on duty would come by and surreptitiously brush it off the table. After a while, we didn't even notice the nuns. I think that was the idea—we were meant to internalize our manners until our actions were seamless."

"Sounds like a finishing school."

"It was that and more. You know, Aladar, I once took a test related to a book about poverty in one of my education classes. I think it was by Ruby Payne. I don't recall the title except it had something to do with poverty. I failed the test in that book miserably not even knowing how to go about getting someone out of jail or how to post bail."

"Why would you know those things?"

"I certainly had no idea how to get a gun or what problems to look for if I bought a used car, and I found the question about grocery stores' garbage bins downright insulting, but I scored high on civilities. I can set a table for twelve with all the silver placed correctly, know how and when to send out invitations, how graciously to accept them or turn them down, how to properly introduce people, send thank you notes, condolences—that kind of thing."

"That accounts for your sense of propriety, excellent taste, and protocol."

"I don't know about that, but I hope I grew out of some of the stereotypes and classism that I held at the university. I don't know how Cathy felt about waiting on us, but I do know we never used it against her. We relied on her for news. One of the reasons she was known as the class gossip was because she heard so much at the tables. We certainly haven't ever brought it up after graduation."

"That was then; this is now," Aladar stated, pouring us another margarita and returning us to the problem at hand. "Did the interrogator ask Cathy how she feels now? These interviewers the department uses are so trained and so good at what they do."

"Yes, he bluntly asked if she was jealous of Angelique."

[127]

"How did she answer that?'

"She admitted she always envied her—her clothes, where she lived, her looks. Angelique is uniquely beautiful in that Barbie-Doll-perfect-features-kind-of-way, as you know, with fiery red hair and green eyes. Aladar, when we went to the Chapel Bar, didn't you notice how even now at her age the men literally stared at her? Whereas Cathy always looked beaten down. Her frazzled hair and pre-mature wattle didn't help either."

"I didn't notice; I only have eyes for you, Dear One."

"Good answer, Aladar, even if I suspect it's a fib."

# Chapter Thirty

Changing the subject, Aladar asked, "Did they question Umbuya?"

"Of course. She was intriguing in a different way—and she was unabashedly forthcoming."

"What do you mean?"

"Let me read her testimony directly from my notes and you'll understand. I want to get her words exact."

I scrolled down to Umbuya's section and shared it with Aladar by reading it aloud.

"As an African, I experience tension not only with other Africans here in America but also with Black Americans.'"

"Can you elaborate, please, Ms. Dumbuya? What do you mean by *tension*."

"Well, if people who look like me are stopped by the police for any number of reasons, it is unlikely we'll be asked if we're from Ghana, Nigeria, Zimbabwe, Atlanta, Haiti, or New York. The police only see a black person."

"Oh, I understand."

"Injustice anywhere to anyone is still injustice," Umbuya explained. "We move in the eyes of many from 'cute' as children to 'interesting' as adolescents to 'threatening' as adults, especially if you are as black as I am or happen to be a male.'"

"Did that attitude affect your relationship with Angelique Forester?"

"Oh, Angelique wasn't like most; she was truly color blind. I never felt she was racist. She was a sweet, unassuming, truly giving person."

"So how did that difference affect you?"

"What do you mean by *difference*?"

[129]

"The way most people respond to you as opposed to the way Angelique responded?"

"In spite of her genuine embrace of my background, I couldn't help but be jealous of her whiteness. I even tried some of the cosmetics that claim they can lighten your skin color, the so-called bleaching creams and brightening serums. For a time, God help me, I wanted to be white, yearned to be white, prayed to be white. As you can see, neither the chemicals nor the prayers worked. But this jealousy was not on Angelique—it was on me," she concluded.

With that I closed my laptop.

"That's powerful," Aladar breathed, "and brave. I guess that leaves Frances..." Aladar began....

"Franny," I interrupted, "always lacked self-esteem even though she was the smartest of us all. She hid behind huge horn-rimmed glasses—even before they were in vogue. She wore her hair as bouffant as possible to distract from her face. She always dressed inconspicuously down, wore brown most of the time, which didn't suit her. She never called attention to herself in any way."

"So, she really disliked Angelique?"

"Franny was incapable of disliking anyone. She was simply a cipher."

"Was she jealous of Angelique?"

"No. She was truly a nonentity."

"That's tragic in another way," Aladar commented.

# Chapter Thirty-One

We had devoured the nachos and ravished the tortillas—not a chip could be found anywhere within our reach. As Aladar poured the remaining almost too-room-temperature margaritas from the pitcher into our glasses, I mused.

"Aladar, I need to check out this Jane person. We have a pretty good handle on everyone else."

"May I help?"

"Maybe. Could you look her up on your end? Find out any background information? Where does she come from? Parents? Schools? That kind of thing?"

"There's a slight charge for poking into the private records of citizens," Aladar said with a wink.

"Oh, dear! You're winking again! And here I am fresh out of funds."

"Well, maybe we can strike a bargain."

"What kind of bargain?"

"A mutually satisfying one."

"Hmmm..."

Chapter Thirty-Two

"Glad you're home; I have news," Aladar said the moment I came through the door.

"I'm glad, too. What's your news?"

"I found some interesting information on this Jane person. But before I share it, I think we need to plan a visit to Sister Agnes."

"Who?"

"Sister Agnes, she's this ancient-as-Methuselah nun who remembers Jane."

"How did you find her? Where is this antediluvian oracle?"

"I found out that Jane lived in an orphanage run by the Sisters of Perpetual Sorrow."

"What a depressing name for an Order of nuns," I commented.

"I know."

"The entire story is depressing. I don't have all the details—that's why I think we need to visit Sister Agnes. Anyway, you're good with nuns. I do better with priests. But I'll give you the broad outlines."

I'm listening."

"Jane came from a moderately wealthy family who had placed her in this Catholic boarding school as a baby, but when she was a little girl, her mother and father were killed tragically in an automobile accident. Without any known relatives coming forth immediately, she was left temporarily in the care of the nuns at that school. Apparently, the thinking was either relatives would be located in due time, or someone would want to adopt a young child—little more than a toddler. There Jane came under wing of this Sister Agnes. I guess they did things differently in those days."

"I guess."

Chapter Thirty-Three

From the Turnpike, we could see the boarding school now an orphanage. Even from this distance, it looked like it belonged in a horror movie. Several turrets jutted from the main frame. I could see their broken wooden finials. I could see balusters with spindles, some decaying, I saw metal plates on the outer walls. No question about it, at one time this 'gingerbread' adorned house, as the Victorians called all that trim, was lovely, but no more.

We rang the bell. "Even it sounds weary," I said to Aladar.

A rather surprisingly spritely nun answered. "You must be Dr. Gallant and Dr. Amory. Sister Agnes is expecting you. Follow me." As she turned, the heavy wooden Rosary Beads that hung from her black leather belt hit against each other emitting a muffled sonorous sound that was unexpected but not unpleasant.

"What is your name, Sister?" I dared.

"I am called Sister Mary Pius," she answered. *Really,* I thought, *a nun named Pius?*

As if reading my thoughts, she clarified, "Pius— the proper noun after the Pope, not a descriptive adjective for me." *Teaches English, I bet,* I thought.

"Please wait here," so before we could engage Sister Mary Pius in further conversation, she ushered us into tiny room with two wooden chairs and a wooden desk and left the room. I felt like I was in detention. Aladar looked like he felt the same way sitting as he did on the edge of that wooden chair.

[134]

Almost immediately Sister Mary Pius returned pushing a wheelchair. Therein sat a woman so old, I doubted she would be helpful. An afghan covered her legs although it was not cold. But if her body seemed frail, her mind proved alert.

"Oh, yes, I remember Jane, Jane Schnake. She was an odd child, a sour child. But who could blame her with her parents so tragically killed and her being abandoned here? I tried to be both mentor and friend, but she proved difficult and moody."

"Could you give me some examples of her moodiness, or how she was sour or difficult, Sister?" I asked.

"Jane was obsessive and reclusive. She began collecting stones when she was first here, hiding them in her room. In the beginning, we indulged her, but soon her room was so filled with them, we had to stop her."

"What then?"

"She moved to collecting dead bugs."

"That we stopped, too. Jane just fixated on things."

"Was she a discipline problem?" Aladar asked.

"No, not really. You may or may not know this, but in its day, this was not an orphanage but a boarding school for wealthy children, children whose parents were busy with their career building.

So, I guess it was when Jane was around eight or so (been here about five or six years hoping for family to find her or to be adopted), Angelique Forester, connected to the Rockefeller and Astor families, came to us. Angelique's family was going through a wicked

[135]

divorce—all over the papers, so they placed her here for a time. A darling child with red hair, green eyes, and a smile for everyone.

"Jane immediately became beguiled by her; she tried everything to be Angelique's friend, monopolized her. But those two couldn't have been more opposite. The other children just gravitated to Angelique. Everyone was her friend. Everyone loved her. On the other hand, no one seemed to even like Jane. And while Angelique wasn't mean to Jane, she really didn't have much in common with someone so dour."

"What happened?"

"Children can be cruel. At first, they tried to befriend her, but she didn't seem interested. Then they tormented her, called her names, that kind of thing. I tried to intervene, to protect her, but I couldn't be by Jane's side all the time. Giving up, the children finally just ignored her—pretending, as only children can do, to not see or hear her at all. They ignored her very being, acted as if she didn't exist. As Shakespeare would phrase it, "that was the most unkindest cut of all."

Did all these nuns teach English? I thought, somewhat surprised by the reference, by its accuracy.

"Did that end it, or did Angelique intervene on behalf of Jane?" I asked, already knowing the answer.

"No and no. *Nothing wrong with this nun's brain. She's sharp,* I thought. "Jane never gave up on trying to be Angelique's friend—nothing dissuaded her. She followed her, did little favors for her, tried to sit by her, saved her a place in line, brought her candy, gave her gifts—and mind you, Jane had very little. Angelique was kind but never really reciprocated."

[136]

"By middle school Jane's obsession with Angelique moved from her to snakes."

"Snakes? Why snakes, Sister?"

"I think it was her last name. The children latched on to it—Schnake. While we nuns gave it the German pronunciation—*Shh* as in 'be quiet' with the second syllable pronounced *ache* like a pain. We pronounced it 'Shh ache'—like *shake*—omitting the *n*, but the children taunted her by adding the *n—snake and the long e sound at the end of the word,* like *snake ee—snakey.* I think they called her that to be mean.

"Did Angelique call her 'Snakey'?"

"I never heard Angelique call her that. Angelique was a giver not a taker, with a big heart. I hated to see her leave. But once the divorce was settled, her father claimed her and took her from us."

"What happened to Jane?"

"Some relatives were finally located. I was told she was foisted upon them. They were unhappy about it not having much money and all, and Jane was unhappy about it, too. That's all I know."

As if on cue, Sister Mary Pius appeared. In that hushed whispered voice of nuns, she said to Sister Agnes, "Sister, you must not overexert yourself. Time for prayers and your nap."

Just as Sister Pius took hold of the wheelchair's handles Sister Agnes leaned over toward us and whispered, "There is one more thing I think you should know, my Dears."

"What is that, Sister?" I asked.

"Once, and only once, mind you, Jane told me she hated Angelique and wanted her dead. I told her to put that thought out of her head. She never said it again, so I thought she obeyed me."

Sister Agnes smiled and nodded to Sister Pius and to Aladar and me, patted my hand, then blessed us both with the sign of the cross before Sister Pius rolled her back to her convent life.

"I think receiving a blessing from such a saintly soul will bring us good luck in this case," I said to Aladar in the car. Aladar rolled his eyes. Still, my heart felt heavy, heavy for all concerned.

Chapter Thirty-Four

Jane thought back over her day, *I can't believe my luck. Angelique stopped me today as I collected the soils. "Jane, how are you?" she began. I stiffened, thinking she either finally recognized me or a complaint was coming. People who live in this building do not interact casually with those of us who work here—unless there is something wrong. Then they find us. All kinds of thoughts ran through my brain when I heard her call my name. Better something I did wrong than being recognized when I was so close to fulfilling my plan. What could I have done wrong? I've been so careful. I don't want to ask outright, so I tried what we maids call the 'underling'approach."*

"I'm good, Ms. Forester. Is there something you need, something I can do for you?"

"You aren't married, are you?"

"No, **ma'am** I'm not."

"So, you don't have any children?"

"No, **ma'am**."

"Are you taking care of an elderly parent or relative?"

"No, **ma'am**."

"To answer your question, then, yes, Jane, there is something you can do for me. I intend to spend some time at my Pocono home, but I'll need a driver to get me there and back plus be my companion while there. My 'usuals' aren't available, and though I sometimes drive myself, I'm not up to it this time. I'll pay you, of course, and make arrangements for someone else to pick up the soils at the high rise while you're gone."

This is too good to be true. Jane thought resisting the urge to pinch herself. *Here I've been mentally devising ways to kill the bitch and she's going to practically pay me to do it! I'll play it cool.*

"I'd love that, but I do have a pet."

"A pet? A sweet kitty or a darling dog?"

"A boa constrictor."

"What? A snake? Is it dangerous?"

"Not at all. Because I was trained in handling, Boa is tame. He lives in a vivarium I had made especially for him. You won't even know he's in the house."

Now it was Angelique's turn to wonder. *Why does she refer to the snake as if 'boa' is its first name and the snake is masculine?*

"This pet is a boa constrictor and you call it by the name 'Boa'?"

"Yes, ma'am."

There stood Angelique Forester actually invitingme and my beloved Boa to her mountain retreat. Ah, the ironies of life. Do things happen for a purpose? Jane continued thinking as she smiled at Angelique. Angelique smiled back.

"Of course, I expect you to work, look after me, do some cooking and cleaning while there, pack beforehand and unpack while there, then repeat the process—pack my stuff to leave," Angelique explained.

"Of course, ma'am," Jane's brain was open full throttle, she thought, *except I won't have to repeat the process if my plan proves fail-safe.*

[140]

"I'd be honored to help you, Ms. Forester, plus I've never been to the Poconos. It will be an adventure." *You can't even imagine how much of an adventure it will be for me, you rich, pompous bitch!*

"It's beautiful in the mountains, Jane, especially now with the leaves turning. Then it's a satisfying arrangement? I'll get back to you with the little details, but do call to have someone from the dealership pick up my car to give it a thorough check-up before we leave. I don't want anything going wrong in the mountains."

"Yes, ma'am."

Once back in her apartment, Jane danced around it thinking, *all these years that uppity bitch thought she was so smart—never admitting she knew me, and all I ever wanted was to be her friend, hang out with her, go to some of those swell places with her—well, she'll soon see.   She never did pay me any mind even in grammar school. By high school, she thought herself above me, thought herself above others, too. Thought of me as an "underclassman" in every sense of the word. Thought of me as 'cellophane Jane." Thought of me as invisible. She'll soon see how invisible I am not.*

She looked down on me when she found out my parents didn't have the money to pay the tuition for that school but had secured work at the school to pay for it—at least until they were killed in that automobile accident and left me there.

Life isn't fair. I had to leave that school. Go live with some poor relatives. Lost track of her. Then she shows up in that high rise while I'm struggling to pay bills. Life definitely isn't fair. But I'm not going to think

[141]

about that now. I'm going to think about my plan for her.

Jane, being neurotically obsessive, among other traits, kept going over and over things in her mind, most of the time she brooded over the same negative things about Angelique.

She pretended to be all goodie-good, but I could see through her. My snakes told me things about her. Best thing I ever did was take Mr. Hoover's herpetology elective in middle school. I didn't even know what herpetology meant at first, but I figured anything was better than another religion class.

I discovered in his class that I liked snakes and they liked me. When Mr. Hoover found that out, he taught me how to handle them—even the venomous ones. He taught be how to milk their venom. I knew that someday that knowledge would help me more than algebra or calculus. Snakes became my curriculum, my religion.

Then I took a class with Ms. MacNamara. I loved her class—all about ancient symbols and such. Ms. MacNamara told us snakes were big symbols and were connected to our pineal glands. That's when I figured out how snakes knew so much. That's when I started talking to my snakes and listening to them.

"Little Angel" thinks that 'Eye of Horus' tattoo she got will protect her from me. I hate that tattoo. I heard her tell someone in the high rise that her 'boyfriend advised it.' Ha! Ha! Ha! Like a tattoo could protect her from my snakes!

I saw it one day when I was in her bathroom collecting the soils from the hamper. She had just stepped out of the shower. She lifted her arm and there in the mirror I saw the puny thing.

My serpents are more powerful than her tattooed 'eye.' SERPENTS ARE GODS! Snakes are shrewd. That's even in the Bible—Matthew or some place. But my favorite is in Genesis. I memorized it. "Now the serpent was more crafty than any of the wild animals the LORD God had made."

Sister Agnes didn't like it when I told her that my serpent was morecrafty than any other animal. Told me to turn my thoughts away from snakes. But I couldn't—didn't want to—won't. I'm going to get rid of that tattoo—my snakes demand it. Get rid of Angelique, too.

Sister Agnes really didn't like it when I told her I wished Angelique was dead. She told me it was a mortal sin and not to think such things. But I did. Still do.

I will make good my promise to Boa, kill Angelique, and take all her beautiful purses—most especially that bejeweled snake clutch. I overheard her tell a friend that the Chinese zodiac inspired it—OMG, I love that one! When I hold it in my hand, I actually feel the power of the snake crawling into me.

Angelique doesn't know I take it out when she's not home and just hold it. I walk around holding it, just holding it—it gives me tingles. Sometimes it gives me more than tingles.

And that couture clutch made out of the skin of the Elaphe snake—I really love that one. I love the way that crystal-embellished serpent slithers across its front. That purse gives me electricity. When I run my hand over the snake on it, I can feel that snake entering my body. It makes me shiver. "Little Angel" probably doesn't

[143]

even know what an Elaphe snake is! She doesn't deserve those things. She doesn't love snakes like I do. Like I love Boa. Like Boa loves me.

Those two pieces alone are worth a fortune and worth this risk I'm taking. With the ransom money I'll be able to buy whatever whenever I want, go where I want, travel in style....

And with those thoughts coiling around in her brain like a snake, Jane danced some more.

Chapter Thirty-Five

Jane arrived at Angelique's exactly on time. "What would you like me to do now, Ms. Forester?" she asked immediately almost curtsying she was so excited. *Let's get this show on the road. Let's get this over with."*

"Good morning, Jane. Thank you for being so prompt. Ah, I'd like you to start packing. I think you should pack my clothes—nothing fancy—we will be in the Poconos where life is so lay back. Take the mountain climb into consideration, too. Choose casual things, things I can layer, comfortable walking shoes, that kind of thing."

"Yes, ma'am."

"Except, Jane, I'd like you to pack some of my prettiest nightgowns and robes. OK? I like to look pretty when I go to bed. Understand?"

"Yes, ma'am. Your prettiest nightwear." *I wonder why she wants those,* Jane thought.

"We'll be gone about two weeks, so think about that, too, won't you, Darling?"

"Yes, ma'am."

"I have a luncheon today; I'll be gone most of the afternoon. Do you think you could have all the packing finished by say three o'clock?"

"Yes, ma'am."

"Have you had my car checked over like I suggested when you agreed to accompany me—gas, oil, all that?"

"Yes, ma'am."

[145]

"Please notify Mr. Muska, the doorman. Tell him I'll be gone two weeks. He'll know what to do."

"Yes, ma'am."

"Oh, and Jane. Are you bringing that vivarium for your snake or have you made other arrangements for it?"

I really hope she's not bringing that monstrosity. I hate snakes and hers is gigantic. And she wants me to believe it's not poisonous. Well, it will stay in that house she's got for it if she brings it. I wouldn't have agreed to her bringing it if I didn't need someone to get me up there and back and to help me.

"I'm bringing Boa. You said I could."

"Not my favorite pet, Jane, but under the circumstances...." Angelique trailed off."

"Boa won't be any bother to you or me," Jane assured her.

That's an odd thing to say, Angelique thought. *But Jane is so quiet, I think her word choice is limited.*

"Do you have any questions, Jane?"

"No, ma'am."

"Good. I'll leave you to the packing, then."

"Yes, ma'am."

Angelique went off to her luncheon where they discussed at great length the details for their reunion. Angelique thought she'd die of ennui when the decision between tiramisu or flan with strawberries for dessert stretched out for over an hour. She could have kissed Franny, ever the arbiter, who finally stepped in with the suggestion, "Let's offer both and then everyone can choose." *I mean, really?* She thought. *I'm so glad I have*

[146]

my business to occupy me, too much of this unproductive fluff and my brain will turn to into mush.

Jane was thinking, too. *I must not waste any time. When we get up in the mountains, I don't want her to get cold feet about Boa once she "lives" with him for a while. My darling Boa can be intimidating to those who don't know him. Scares most people, ignorant people who are afraid of all snakes. Can't tell one snake from the other. Besides, I have to come up with some reason pretty fast to cause a fight with her, so I can knock her out and then execute my plan. She thinks her tattoo will protect her. Ah the irony!*

After Angelique left, Jane retrieved Boa from the vivarium, she began her ritualistic handling, which she called 'crooning,' "Come here my thirteen-foot beauty. Come wind yourself around your mama. Come crawl over my body, over, around, and between my legs. See how good it feels."

As the boa felt the warmth of Jane's body, it continued to wriggle and writhe on top of her. "Oh, my glorious long one, we will soon be together forever with no interruptions. Angelique thought she could separate us, she was angry with me when she first saw us together, jealous of you, of us, I know, but now she's pretending having you visit here is fine. She doesn't fool us, though, does she, Boa? I will take care of her. Your cousin from Australia has arrived. She will be milked. Her venom will kill Angelique and Angelique will be jealous no longer."

With that, Jane laid back on the sofa and continued her crooning.

[147]

Chapter Thirty-Six

Everything went swimmingly for the first two days in the mountains. Angelique busied herself with a balance design she had conjured while visiting her friend, Elaine.

Although Elaine was elderly and quite agile, she used a walker forbalance. As Angelique watched her bump into this counter or get caught on the corner of that chair, she imagined a walker that would enable Elaine and other seniors to avoid such obstacles with grace and dignity. Angelique couldn't wait to get to her office in her mountain retreat to sketch it and work it out. The mountains inspired her.

Jane didn't bother her. *She's perfect—unobtrusive, invisible,* Angelique thought—only asking if Angelique wanted something to eat or drink as snacks or what she wanted to eat at mealtimes. Occasionally Jane asked if she needed anything else. Angelique tried not to think about the boa.

But Jane was busy, devising a plan to get Angelique in a good, old-fashioned cat fight.

I have to make her angry, very angry. Maybe arrange things so she sees me actually stealing something, something she cares about—one of her purses. With one of those in my hand, I can swing around and club her with it. Those little metal purses are hard and heavy enough to knock her out if I swing right. Maybe not engage her in a fight. I'll just knock her out and go from there.

Jane went over and over and over her plan, revising it as if she were working on a script for a Broadway play.

Once I've got her knocked out cold and down on the ground, I'll get the snake and let it bite Angelique—or maybe I'll bite her again—now there's an idea! Then suddenly Jane thought the plan with Boa was too iffy—*Boa might not bite, might not bite Angelique; might not bite her tattoo.*

Boa has to bite Angelique on that tattoo otherwise my resentment won't go away. I know that about myself. I know what I'll do. I'll put the venom of that Inland Taipan into a syringe and inject it. The neurotoxins will parallelize precious Angel. I won't call anyone right away. Make sure Angelique's out even though that injection will kill her within minutes. When I finally call the police, I'll be all upset, pretend I was somewhere else in the house and didn't find her for over an hour or so. That's all possible. That's all plausible.

I want the police to find some bruises, think a burglar did it, so I'll rough her up a bit and then set her all up as if nothing happened, all pretty like. I'm younger and in better shape than she is, so that shouldn't be a problem—plus I'll be taking her by surprise.

[149]

# Chapter Thirty-Seven

Aladar was uncharacteristically late coming home from his office. I had planned a lovely evening, prepared his favorite African food, wore my sexiest dashiki.

Then my phone pinged. I wanted to ignore it, let it go to message so I could finish my preparations, but I thought *he might be calling to explain his tardiness.* Then when I saw the caller on the ID, I picked up immediately.

"Cathy? What a surprise! What's going on?"

"There's been a shooting at Angelique's place in the mountains."

"What?"

"The police just issued a statement. Turn on your TV." And with that Cathy clicked off.

# ChapterThirty-Eight

I immediately turned on the news.

...Forester, who has been missing for the past two weeks, was found today in her Pocono Mountain mansion. An unidentified body was also found. Pennsylvania authorities are not releasing any further information at this time. Tune it for more news at ....

Just then Aladar walked through the door. I fairly screamed, "Oh, my goodness! Aladar!"

"What is it?" He fairly screamed back.

"Angelique has been found. She's okay but another body was also found in her home. Cathy just called me. She told me the TV News claims someone was shot in Angelique's mountain home."

"Let me run to the office. I'll get all the info I can get. I had a call earlier but chose to ignore it since you spent the day at the precinct, and I was in and out all day. I didn't think it was urgent."

"I want to go with you. Let me change. I can't go like this—not in a dashiki."

Looking me over with approval in his eyes, Aladar agreed, "No, no you can't, but by all means, change back when we get home."

Chapter Thirty-Nine

Once back homeagain we shed our coats but we couldn't shed the sadness of this case. They didn't know much at the precinct. We tried but all we could definitely ascertain was an unidentified woman was dead, and Angelique was in trauma. I put my dashiki back on, but even all the colors in its ironically titled 'Angelina print' didn't help my mood or Aladar's.

He began making our favorite cocktails as I began making some snacks, but neither of us felt hungry or thirsty for that matter.

I caught Aladar's arm in mid-cocktail-shake as I quoted, "'And they, since they were not the ones dead, turned to their affairs.' Frost got it right, didn't he? We have no alternative now but to go on with life. We feel sadness for the woman and for Angelique, but in reality, we can't do anything about it."

"Except try to solve this case. And we're lucky to be able to share that purpose with each other."

Rather mechanically we went through the motions of having our drinks, eating our dinner, watching some TV, and going to bed. Aladar reached for me almost at the same moment I reached for him. "Why is this case touching us so deeply, besides the fact that Angelique was a friend?" I mumbled.

He thought for a few moments and then said, "because it underscores the fact that life is a crap shoot."

[152]

# Chapter Forty

This time as we drove to Angelique's, we didn't comment on the leaves turning— didn't even notice them. We didn't put on the car's massage—didn't even think of it. We didn't talk either—didn't seem to have much to say.

Finally, I said, "Aladar, who would want to try to kill somebody so sweet, so giving a woman as Angelique? And who is this unidentified woman and why kill her?"

"Maybe things went awry. It's got to be jealousy, Elizabeth. Or maybe the murderer wanted the suspicion to rest on Angelique. She has so much. And all of what she had is the finest, most expensive."

"True enough, but she didn't flaunt it. She didn't waste it. She never rubbed anyone's noses in it. Yet the solid suspects are most probably innocent. Could this murder have been something chancy? Someone out there in the mountains hiding? An escaped convict we haven't heard about yet? A nut case? Something or someone out-of-the-blue like we talked asked about earlier? Could it have been the Fates? Something that just happenedthere where her so-called 'cabin' is so isolated? Something or someone weird?"

"Could have been any one of those things. We won't know until we examine her and the site."

"This drive today seems interminable," I commented after a while, impatience in my voice.

"That's always the way when you are anticipating the outcome."

"I think that's profound, Aladar. I think you are right, but I think that holds true for more than a drive to somewhere or circumstances such as this."

"Go on."

"I remember waiting to go to a birthday party; it seemed the day would never come. Or waiting for the proverbial pot to boil when I cooked something, especially if I had guests. Or sitting in the waiting room during Du's last operation, thinking I would never hear the results, yet fearing them. I knew the doctor would inevitably appear, but I sat there hoping yet dreading the inevitable all the same. Time froze. True, it's all about anticipating the end."

We both sighed, inched closer to each other, filled as we were with the moment, the realization, the truth of it.

Chapter Forty-One

We arrived at Angelique's amid squad and unmarked cars, ambulances, mobile care units, TV station vehicles, and many knots of nosy neighbors. People stood looking around as if they had business at this site or as if waiting for directions for what they should do next.

"Where did all these people come from?" I asked Aladar somewhat rhetorically. "I thought this was an isolated section of the Poconos."

"Apparently not," came his answer.

Barricades sat around the outside of the house like skinny horses expecting riders to jump upon them and ride into the sunset. Typical yellow crime scene barrier tape and rope cordoned off the area. We passed under both the tape and rope.

It was then I felt a slight breeze. *It's truly fall. There's a hint of death in the wind. Seems like yesterday when we celebrated Gladys' wedding—strange what you notice when in a heightened state,* I thought. *Strange, too, how quickly life changes.*

A fellow I didn't know ran over to greet Aladar, hand and arm extending in mid run. "Damnedest thing, Al, the dead woman looks so peaceful just lying there flat on the floor, arms outstretched like wings as if she's a bird about to fly away."

"Where is Angelique?" Aladar asked.

Max almost babbled, "Ms. Forester's there, too, all dressed up for bed. By the way, she's awake but almost catatonic. But, hell, Al, she's one beautiful

[155]

woman, I'd say. We figure she was meant to be the target. But why would anyone want to kill someone so beautiful? 'Course I'm a sucker for redheads—always was. I'm glad the murderer was unsuccessful as far as she's concerned."

But, shaking his head as if to admonish himself for getting into his personal preferences, he muttered, "We need to focus our forensics on the dead woman."

"Take us to where you found them," Aladar requested. Nodding his head in my direction and steering me toward the man whose hand remained extended, Aladar introduced us. "Elizabeth, this is Dr. Max Helmn, a fellow forensic scientist. I work with him every day. Max, this is Dr. Elizabeth Armory, my assistant."

Max immediately grasped my hand and shook it. "Oh, so you're the lady sleuth I've heard so much about!" Then he flashed a big smile, "I'm pleased to meet you."

"Likewise."

We continued to exchange pleasantries as we followed Max who led us to the back master bedroom, a huge room befitting this huge misnamed 'cabin.' At first glance it did look like Angelique was in the act of preparing to retire, but upon closer examination, the entire scene struck me as too still—like a still life painting, too inert, too staged. It felt like a movie set waiting to spring into action, waiting for the director to arrive, waiting to hear "lights, action, camera."

Angelique seemed drugged—totally out of it. She sat just so as if positioned by a stage crew who

[156]

perhaps had perfectly positioned everything in the room.

She sat upright, propped against the back of her cyan heart-shaped boudoir chair in front of a large mirror encased in gold. I had a flashback to the Chapel Bar. Both she and the chair looked uncharacteristically out-of-place against the rustic paneling and the countrified feel of this place. I wanted to move her to that posh bar where we last talked, or into a palace, or at the very least back to her high-rise home.

She had her right hand on the handle of a silver hairbrush that lay on the vanity in front of her as if she just reached for it. Her left hand rested lightly on the chair's seat as if she might be about ready to stand. I bumped the seat ever so slightly and saw that eye tattoo again, like some kind of an omen. *Was it a good a bad luck omen?* I asked myself.

Her pale pink robe was slightly askew, but modestly so. She wore those forties' bedroom slippers, the kind made of satin with a puff of faux feathers in front like a powder puff, the kind with low heels for comfort but also for style. They matched her robe and gown in that 40s kind of way. She looked like a bride on her wedding night. I almost looked for the groom.

I asked myself, *Why would she get dressed so fancy only to slip into bed alone, out here? What am I missing?* But then her Grand Auntie Florence's advice popped into my brain, "always wear beautiful bedroom attire." *Of course*, I thought.

The other woman was spread eagle on her stomach on the floor, her face flat against the wood. Shot, at first look. That Glock resting next to her—again

[157]

looked like a prop in a movie set. The entire scene was bizarre, a tableau. The scene reminded me of the dioramas I made in shoeboxes as a kid.

The medics came to remove Lady X and to examine Angelique. Aladar began doing his thing, so I wandered about.

Entering the master bathroom, a gallery of photographs greeted me. Judging by their gloss or fade, I figured these captured Angelique's life since childhood.

Interestingly, I found one with Mary, pale and thin, and little (I barely recognized her)—the alleged sister. She awkwardly heldup Angeliqueby herarms as Angelique, a baby barely able to stand, tried to balance on her tiptoes in front of the ever-so-slightly taller Mary. Directly behind Mary stood a man with a black bushy mustache. I looked for other pictures of Mary and the man.

The photograph that most caught my eye was apparently taken at the zoo. Both girls stood in front of a notice that read: VENOMOUS SNAKES. No sign of an adult.

That struck me as odd. *Why would anyone pose two little girls in such a dangerous place? What message was the person who took the photo trying to convey?* Then I dismissed my thought as perhaps overthinking the situation. *Most probably and most logically that's where they happen to be when it occurred to someone to take the photo.*

When I finished my wanderings, I was convinced Angelique intended a tryst of some sort up here in her mountain home, more specifically in her bedroom. With whom? For what purpose? I could find no evidence to

[158]

contradict my theory; but, much to my chagrin, I could find no evidence to support it either. Upon returning to the bedroom, I overheard Aladar saying,

"Lady X has *algor mortis*."

"What does that mean?" I asked as if I had never left the room.

"It means she hasn't begun to stiffen with *rigor mortis*. Her body is still warm. My educated guess is that she's been dead less than four hours."

"What happens next?" I asked.

"Her body will become more and more rigid. Lividity will set in so the skin will take on a bright red tone that changes to blue or purple. After that, *autolysis* starts. In layman's terms that means the body bloats and decays. Blessedly she isn't at that point yet. We just need to get her to the morgue."

"Be that as it may—the fact remains—Angelique Forester is alive but out of it. Who drugged her? Set her up? Who is this other woman?" Max stated, perplexity clear in his voice.

I offered an alliterative echo, "Yes, who did these dastardly deeds?"

# Chapter Forty-Two

The ride back from the Poconos to our Brownstone seemed even more endless than our ride over. I wondered if we were still filled with anticipation. I didn't feel anticipatory. I felt dulled and somewhat defeated. I couldn't make any of the pieces of this jigsaw puzzle crime fit. It felt like someone had taken several puzzles and randomly mixed all the pieces together. I felt flummoxed.

"Aladar?" I asked him while patting his thigh in a familiar way. Aladar smiled broadly. "How can you smile like that after seeing such a scene?"

"Let me just explain by pointing out that your hand is in exactly the best spot."

"Aladar!" I exclaimed, quickly withdrawing my hand, "how can you even be thinking such things at a time like this?"

"Easy, Elizabeth. Like I said, your hand was in exactly the best spot."

"You are irredeemable."

"But you are intractable."

"You are obdurate."

"But you are wonderful," with that Aladar leaned over to plant a kiss directly on my cheek. BINGO!" he cried out.

"Oh, do be serious. You'll run us off the road."

"I am being serious. We are in a serious business. What does your fascinating brain tell us about this crime so far?"

"I think Angelique had arranged a tryst."

[160]

"You think she had a secret lover? Do you think the woman on the floor was her secret lover? Or maybe the unidentified woman was enraged because Angelique was seeing her husband, or maybe she was just a friend," Aladar was thinking out loud.

"I don't know, but she had something going. What I'm trying to understandis if any of this connects to the two notes she received. Everything seems such an odd sequence of events."

Aladar agreed.

"I also find it odd that so social a woman would want to meet anyone up in the mountains. Who was she trying to avoid in the City? What 'eyes'did she want to keep at bay? She certainly had the means to get a hotel room. New York City is a big place. She knows it well. She could easily get lost in the City if she wanted to. If she wanted a tryst, the City would be an easy place to get lost. And staying in the City would be more convenient than trucking up to the mountains."

"And there's an eye reference again," Aladar pointed out.

"Hmm...By the way, Aladar, who found Angelique?"

"Jane. She brought Jane with her."

"Jane?" I muttered in surprise. "The invisible Jane who slips in and out of Angelique's home like a shadow? She certainly adds another piece to this puzzle."

"That very Jane."

"Was that Jane on the floor?" I asked suddenly aware of the same skinny frame, the same mousy-colored hair that hid even a profile of her face.

"I think so, but we won't know until all the investigating is over. If the unidentified woman is Jane, she looked decidedly different sprawled on that floorthan she did at the precinct."

"Aladar, I just noticed you are not on the road home. Where are we going?"

"You'll soon see."

Twisting among the trees that grew so profusely in the mountains, Aladar drove for a short while longer. This was all very mysterious. I thought he was about to show me something connected to this case. I thought he knew of a clue hidden among the rocks or trees. Then suddenly we came upon a sign pointing East that read: 'Lover's Rock Retreat.'

"What's this?"

"I'm abducting you!"

"You scoundrel! I shall report you to the authorities!"

"Go right ahead, my Dear Sleuth, but you will find no phones or means here in these secluded woods for outside human contact. And, thinking ahead, I have hidden your cell phone. I shall have you all to myself."

"I have no suitable clothes," I protested.

"Perla packed your suitcase. I have it in the trunk."

"You are a diabolical 'planner a-header'! And to think you are in cahoots with my beloved Perla! I shall fire her the moment I return."

"What makes you think you'll be returning? This case is far from solved. We have more investigating up here to do."

"Schemer! I shall scream!"

[162]

"No one will hear you. This cabin is truly isolated."

"Aladar Gallant, you have a devious mind."

With that Aladar eased the car to a stop in front of a charming-looking bungalow, retrieved me from my seat, and carried me the few steps to its front door. *I feel like a bride,* I thought.

As he gently let me down, he kissed me, opened the door, slipped off his jacket and mine, and led me to the bedroom. "I want you to check it out."

It was typical Poconos—unassuming but comfortable, simple but inviting. I noticed a bottle of Chalk Hill with two glasses on the dresser.

"Check it out for what reason?" I asked, feigning ignorance.

"Oh! I don't know—maybe to see if these digs will do for the night."

"Now you are diabolical, devious, *and* lascivious," I accused him.

"You know how word play excites me."

"And you are a lech, debauching an innocent lady."

"Wait until you see the bathroom."

And with that Aladar swept me into an adjoining room. There I saw the jacuzzi. The rim of which was a garish red, emphasizing its heart-shape. The tub itself was at least double, maybe triple, a regular size tub. "Aladar, we shall drown," I protested, looking at the kitschy jacuzzi that tried so hard to be chic.

"Then we shall join all the water sprites and rollick with them."

"Did Perla pack my bathing suit?"

[163]

"Why?" was the last word I heard before we slipped into the lustful petting and moved directly to that level of pure aesthetic drunkenness called passion. *Who needs wine?* I thought. *Who needs a tempting tub? And for that matter, who needs a bathing suit?* I was only aware of the power of love that this being was bequeathing upon me—over and over again.

Chapter Forty-Three

We sat in the large open space called the 'Great Room'in the advertisements of the cozy 'cabins' in the Poconos, not crammed into a stifling room at the precinct.The investigative team, reporters, Angelique, who recovereda little from her trauma,and who insisted upon attending, and me. With our very own "Inspector Cluedo"(my nickname for Aladar) aka Inspector Gallant, asking questions, I hoped they would lead to a big Eureka! The revelation of the doer of the deed! The realization and the murderer!

Would Aladar call in a surprise witness as he did in our last case when he sprung Dr. Henson upon us? Or does he have surprising evidence none of us have yet seen? Was Angelique really the intended victim? Does this connect to her threatening notes? If so, how?"

I, the Dr. Amory—not the Dr. Henson or Dr. Watson—to Dr. Gallant's Sherlock Holmes, if I may mix not my metaphors but my detectives, was along to "employ *abduction*," as Aladar put it. *I hope I can ferret out the solution using my abductive-reasoning brain. Who is the obvious killer? What conspicuous clue am I missing?*

"Rattataatat," I leaned over and breathed only loud enough for Aladar's ears.

"Angelique wasn't gunned down," Aladar hastened to remind me back in a whisper. "She was seated upright, seemingly drugged, ready to brush her hair," he reminded me.

"Emphasis on the 'tat,'" I said. I'm creating word play with onomatopoeia for my brain. A bit of drama excites my neurons," I whispered back.

"Someone had placed that Glock 17 next to her chest. It had been fired once, but that didn't kill her," Max was explaining the position of the Glock as if we all couldn't see it. The Glock had only been fired once—but not at Angelique.

"What did?" one of the local reporters asked.

"What did what?"

"Kill her?"

"Kill who?"

"The dead VIC."

"Dude, the prelim look suggests venom."

"Venom? Boy! That's a new one," the young reporter said.

I bet this is his first assignment, I thought.

"And the VIC seems to be the woman on the floor, aka, a person named 'Jane,' who drove Ms. Forester here," Max said.

"I would like to call your attention to two things," I announced. Everyone stirred a bit but listened up. *I guess my reputation as Grand Auntie of Sleuthdom precedes me,* I thought, rather pleased. "Angelique had an eye tattoo on her left arm, which she recently had covered up with another larger, more garish tat."

"What did it look like?" asked the young reporter whose name we discovered was Benjamin Briton; his colleagues called him BB, as in the gun. "She was taken away before I got here."

Lesson learned, BB, I thought, *if you want the full story, get to the crime scene early.*

[166]

"The original tat was a black stylized version of the left eye called 'The Eye of Horus,' I said.

"This particular tattoo shows the pupil attached to the top lid, so there is a bit of space beneath it—between it and the bottom lid, that is. Under the bottom lid there is a curlicue line. On top of the eye, there is a slice of eyebrow." I hoped the reporter had a keen visual ability or was taking detailed notes.

"Was there any color?"

"Not on the original tattoo just black ink."

"What about the cover up tat?"

"The cover up is fresh, larger, wider, and more colorful. People often embellish an original tat, changing it to avoid the pain of having it removed. If they have a reason for eradicating its original purpose or any memory of the original, they often camouflage it."

"Do you think that was the case here?"

"Yes, I do. The newer more elaborate embellishment features a bird with long wide wings holding the eye. The eye is green then outlined in a light yellow with other colors surrounding it."

I continued, "This Eye of Horus, was a revered religious concept during the Egyptian era. You can find all manner of replications on ancient tombs, burial places, amulets, and jewelry. Even today, it holds many meanings from recent gang symbols to denotations and connotations dating back to that ancient world of the Egyptians."

"Where is it on her arm?" Everyone asked almost in unison, sounding surprised about the tattoo.

[167]

Apparently, no one had noticed it—but now found it immensely curious.

"On that fleshy part of her left arm between the shoulder and elbow—on the inside. That area of our anatomy is called the axilla. Butits position is not the only issue;I also want you to notice something else, something more interesting."

"What?" Max asked, beginning to sound impatient.

"A bite mark on that eye, on that tattoo, or more accurately—over it—like the biter—a human, I think—wanted to bite the tat off."

"Now's when I like being in forensics," Max said. I could almost see him salivating."Women bite when they fight," he offered. "Men don't do that. Or," he reluctantly added, clearly liking his first interpretation better, "maybe it could have been some animal out here."

"I thought the same thing, Max, so I researched it. You are correct, women typically bite when they fight, but the lab will have to analyze it before we rule on it or rule out an animal bite."

Just then, Aladar spoke up, "That there is a bite is a fact inour favor. Bite marks are like dental fingerprinting, especially a human's bite. Human dentition is unique—even identical twins leave different teeth impressions. That bite mark is as good as a calling card."

"That's good news, Al. So, we'll know who done it pretty soon?" BB asked giving voice to what everyone else was thinking, hoping.

[168]

I spoke up, decisively, "Forensic odontology is powerful as Dr. Gallant has reminded us.In this case it will confirm who murdered our unidentified woman and harassed Angelique Forester—or—who intended to murder Angelique.

# Chapter Forty-Four

"When do you see the detective in charge of this case?" Aladar asked me when we were once again back at the Brownstone.

"Tomorrow morning," I responded.

"Do you want me to go with you?"

"Of course, but before that I want to talk through my reasoning. You know I'm an oral problem solver. I want to be sure I have all the ends tied nice and tidy."

"Let me fetch us some wine. We can sip as you tell all."

"Excellent."

Aldar poured two glasses of my favorite Chardonnay. Nicely iced, it sat perfectly on my tongue.

"I'll begin with the obvious, Aladar.I started my thinking by asking myself: Who was the most likely suspect? Dismissing the six of us as without motive unless one of us wanted one or all of those Isabelle Fayette's, which, I bet we all do, but wouldn't kill for them, and thinking that unlikely because given each woman's financials, those could be purchased. You know, Aladar, anything can be purchased for the right price—well, almost everything." I paused to catch my breath. "That left the doorman, Mary, and Jane, and I suppose the man with the bushy black mustache."

"Go on."

"I dismissed the doorman based on the stationery. I remembered one of the forensic scientists on your team saying that the stationary most likely belonged to a woman, a wealthy woman who could afford such a luxury. That fact alone disqualified the doorman. But that triggered the Aristotelean quote I love: '*A likely impossibility is always preferable to an unconvincing possibility.*'"

"That a woman chose that stationery seemed to me more a likely impossibility than an unconvincing possibility of it being a man's choice or just happen stance.

"How didyou figure that?"

"What is the chance the murderer owned the same stationery as that owned by the murdered woman?

"That conclusion was reinforced when your team discovered it's a custom design, available in stores frequented by a particular echelon. I'm betting someone pilfered that stationery directly from Angelique."

"And the handwriting?"

"None of the suspects gave us a possible match. So, I took another look at the two women. Mary, the sister, and Jane, the shadow. Who was most likely? I reasoned it had to be Mary since we know next-to-nothing about Jane. And Mary seems to have every reason to be jealous of Angelique."

"That means you whittled the suspects to Mary and Jane? What about the man with the mustache?" Aladar asked.

"Yes, I have, and I have a theory about the man. When we visited the so-called cabin, which is really a mansion in the mountains, and I wandered around, I saw groupings of candid photographs in one of the

[171]

baths—of all places—of family photos takenover time. Mary was on an early photo with a man with a mustache."

"So?"

"I reasoned that must have been taken when Mary and her mother were still in the father's good graces. I studied the man. He was well groomed, mustache trimmed in the style of the time, well dressed."

"The father of Mary?"

"The father of Mary *and* Angelique."

"How did you reason that?"

"I didn't just reason that, Aladar, I found proof. When we were in the initial stages of this investigation, Mr. Muska, the doorman, told us a man, claiming to be Angelique's father, came to see her. But Mr. Muska insisted he was a different man than the one Angelique had earlier introduced him to as her father. Bells went off. Remember: Mr. Muska said, 'I'm good at remembering faces.'"

"You are amazing."

"First, I checked the mustached man's ID with the receptionist at the high rise who had been made aware we were working on the case. Then I trucked down to the Surrogate's Courthouse."

"And?"

"He checked out as Angelique's father *and* Mary's father. Angelique's mother had both girls by the same man."

"Then who was that first man Mary's mother introduced as the father?"

"I'm guessing he either worked for Astor or was another man Mary's mother was seeing at the time. It's that pride thing again. Save face. But the fact remains—Angelique and Mary are blood sisters—not sisters-in-law or half-sisters."

"Are you sure of that?"

"Mary verified that before her mother died, she told Mary that Angelique was her sister. That caused Mary to hatch a plan to work for Angelique, ingratiate herself to Angelique for many reasons—most of them monetary, knowing that her sister was sweet and giving."

"That sounds like sibling jealousy on steroids," Aladar commented, "But why not just tell Angelique? Clear the air once and for all. Why all the machinations?"

"Frankly, Aladar, I think Mary didn't think Angelique would believe her. Besides Mary's mother had tried that tactic with the father, tried to be direct, reason with him, but he'd have none of it, flatly denying any relationship to Mary. He even threatened her. My guess is Mary witnessed it all and figured telling Angelique would get her nowhere. That's when she decided upon subterfuge. That's also when she paid a visit to the Surrogate's Courthouse—wanting proof, no doubt."

"So, it's Mary?"

"Later photos in that bathroom gallery display the same man holding Angelique, walking with her. There is one photo that shows her piggy-backing on his shoulders. Both are smiling broadly. It looks like they

[173]

may have been hiking, picnicking, or swimming. There is no sign of Mary."

Aladar said, "Knowing she wasn't preferred or even accepted is probably another reason Mary decided against a frontal confrontation. Mary may not have had much formal education, but she was smart—what some call 'street smart.'"

"Then I spotted a picture of Angelique in a white lacey dress and veil fit for a religious event such as Holy Communion, prayer book and rosary beads in hand. Another picture captures her in a cap and gown. That one could have been a high school graduation photo. Itprobably was taken in a studio. The same man appears in both those pictures, standing by her side, arm around her waist, smiling."

"You are Grand Auntie, sleuth personified!"

"When I had that much figured, I called Mary, knowing she was talkative. She reiterated what she had told the interrogator. Told me she had nothing to hide. Told me her mother told her that her father was rich but didn't want her. Abandoned both Mary and her mother. Once he saw Mary was born with that withered arm (did you notice it, Aladar?) he said he didn't want a deformed child. Mary started crying into the phone as she repeated that, even after all these years."

"I'm sure that's a painful memory."

"Yes, but the memory didn't deter Mary. She kept talking even through the tears, telling me how her father told her mother he wouldn't accept 'that little freak' under any circumstance and that 'she better get over it.'"

[174]

"'Ma did, but I didn't. I swore I'd get even some day.' When Mary told me that, I concluded the murderer was Mary."

"Aladar, apparently this man threw his money and affection on his little Angel—Angelique—and basically ignored and disowned Mary. Sad, isn't it?"

"It is, but how does rejection and sadness so many years ago figure into this present-day murder?"

"I'm getting to that."

"Before her mother died, actually on her deathbed, her mother reconfirmed to Mary that Angelique was her sister. But it was anticlimactic as Mary long since had authenticated what she had been too young to remember all the details when her mother first told her. When Mary grew older and confirmed what had happened, she became preoccupied with her sister."

"Sister's jealousy?"

"What else? But after her mother passed away, as I told you, Mary contrived a plan to work for Angelique. She was already engaged in domestic work (having had neither the money nor the inclination for any advanced training or college, although sadly I think she has the mind). Nevertheless, it took her years and much finagling to secure that position with the Foresters. Mary was tenacious, though, persisting until she landed a position through a maid service at the high rise."

At that moment, the doorbell rang. Reluctant to answer it, we sat in silence. Then I received a text: **Please answer your door. This is an AMA POSTAL delivery I have something for you.**

[175]

That seemed odd, so we kept our phones in our hands as security while Aladar cracked open the door. There stood a man in brown holding something.

"Yes?"

He thrust a package into Aladar's chest, grumbling, "I'm sorry about this. I don't usually deliver packages this way, but today's been a busy day, and with the spike in crime in this area, I didn't want to just leave it."

"No problem," Aladar said. "Thank you."

We opened the package immediately. "Aladar! This is the missing piece Angelique told us about. It's *arecherché* Fabergé, very rare and very valuable; wemust inform the police we have it and return it to Angelique."

"Who sent it? Is there any name or address anywhere? What about a postmark? Or a better question, why did someone send it to us?" Aladar asked.

"That piece is worth a great deal of money," I restated unnecessarily to the wall, not even attempting to answer his questions.

"Whoever had this piece is probably the killer," Aladar conjectured.

"At the very least, the thief," I said.

"A contrite thief, it seems," Aladar said.

This case now had pieces of the puzzle falling into place. We had a dead body, who was identified; several notes on expensive stationery, which we knew had been stolen from Angelique; and a missing rare item that had been returned. All we needed was the murderer.

[176]

# Chapter Forty-Five

We didn't have any luck tracing the sender of the package. Apparently since we were getting close to the Christmas season and other holidays, AMA POSTAL was backlogged and not as fastidious about checking everything as they usually are.

"Well, at least we can get this Fabergé to Angelique where it belongs," I consoled myself. The time had come for me to report to the detective in charge of this murder. I had played and replayed the entire event multiple times in my head, orally ran it by Aladar several times. I was ready. Or at least I thought I was ready, having vacillated between Mary and Jane several times. But I had one niggling thought *how and why would the killer murder Jane if Angelique was the intended VIC?* I had my abductive reasoning, but no proof.

I picked up my cell phone to call the detective assigned to the case—whose name, interestingly, was Peter Whimsey. I wondered as I waited for him to answer my call, if he realized his name was so close to the British gentleman detective Lord Peter Wimsey, who solved crimes for his own amusement.

"Yes, Detective Whimsey? This is Elizabeth Armory. You may remember I am working on the Forester case with Dr. Aladar Gallant." ....

"Thank you. I have a favor. I was scheduled to meet with you today, but wonder if we could postpone that meeting a few days? ....

"Why?"

"Well, I have a couple of strings still hanging that I'd like to tidy them up and tie everything with a bow before we meet." ....

"A week hence? That is most generous of you, Sir. I am quite sure I'll have all my proverbial ducks in a row and all those strings tied for you by then. Thank you. Have a good day."

# Chapter Forty-Six

"Aladar, do you know that snake farm out there on Highway 145?"

"Yes, it's been there for years. Why?"

"I want to pay Peter Sneg a visit. He's the owner."

"Today?"

"Yes. But first I have to call him to be sure he'll be in. I touched the numbers on my phone for the snake farm, "Mr. Sneg, my name is Elizabeth Armory. I'm a colleague of Dr. Aladar Gallant, who is with the OCME Department of Forensic Biology which operates the largest public DNA crime lab in the world. We are detectives following a murder case. We'd like to pick your brain about a couple of things pertaining to this case; we have some questions about snakes." ....

"No, Sir, you are not in any trouble. We just need information. May we come by and interview you?"

"Today at 2:00 will be perfect." ....

If I thought the room in the precinct was claustrophobic, the room where we sat now, in what I facetiously called the 'SNAKES 'R US' building, made that room seem cavernous. Beside, above, and under us were cages filled with various reptiles. Surrounding us were beady little eyes.

"I hope our reptilian friends don't disturb you, Dr. Armory," Mr. Sneg said.

"Not in the least," I lied.

"And you, Dr. Gallant?"

"I love all beasts," he lied, too.

"Good. With that bit of housekeeping out of the way, how may I help you?"

Housekeeping? I thought, *now there's a wrong word choice if I ever heard one,* but I said, "We need information on snakes for a case."

"No problem. Try me."

"Can average people milk snakes? Would they know how? Would they know how to keep the milk untainted?" I began.

"Let's take those questions one at a time. First, with minimal training most anyone can milk a snake. But it does take some instruction and practice to do it accurately without harming the snake or the person doing the milking. Usually, herpetologists or ophiologists perform that task. It calls for care and a sterile environment. Any 'milk,' which is actually the venom extracted from a snake, should be frozen if it is not used within a reasonable time."

"How long does the venom stay active—if that's the right word?"

"Venom usually keeps its toxicity up to a month."

"Mr. Sneg, what is the difference between snake poison and snake venom?"

"Poison is ingested; venom is injected. But the danger lies in the venom."

"So you swallow poison, but you get a shot of venom?" Aladar asked.

"That's one way to put it," Mr. Sneg answered.

"Where does snake venom come from?"

[180]

"Snakes produce their venom in their salivary glands. They store venom in their large glands before ejecting it out their fangs."

"So, it's the fangs that are milked?" Aladar asked.

"Yes, the venom drips from their fangs. Depending upon the snake and its toxicity, this venom can affect the tissues, organs, muscles, or it can cause hemorrhages for the person receiving it."

I stepped in, "If someone is injected with toxic snake venom and there is no intervention, how long does it take for that person to succumb to the venom? In other words, how long does it take for that person to actually die?"

"Usually, it takes between six and forty-eight hours, but if there's an allergy involved or if the victim is sickly or has a compromised immune system, which always complicates things, demise may follow more quickly."

"I think that concludes our urgent questions, Mr. Sneg," Aladar said. "May we call you if others emerge as we work on this case?"

"Of course, now please allow me to give you my card and a tour of our establishment."

"Thank you."

Chapter Forty-Seven

"Interesting chap, didn't you think Elizabeth?" Aladar asked as we slid into his vehicle ready to drive up once again into the mountains.

"I prefer 'odd duck'. I could have done without the tour. I fear it will give me nightmares—all those eyes, fangs, scales, and slithering.You would think snakes wouldn't bother me as they play such a prominent role in literature from Cadmus in *Metamorphoses* to Emily Dickinson's 'A Narrow Fellow in the Grass' as well as in other classics."

"In your defense, Elizabeth, I'd say snakes in literature are more distant than those we experienced today."

"True. I studied them that way, from a distance, but today they were a bit too close for my taste. Most of the time in literature, snakes symbolize something no good or someone up to no good. That's all I could think about during that horrid tour—evil." Here I shuddered.

"Perhaps that calls for a change of scenery and some liquid refreshment to calm you. We could follow that with a hearty meal to steady your nerves?" Aladar suggested.

"Nothing like a drive with a built-in massage, little vodka, and good food to wipe awayimages of anything unpleasant," I agreed.

"Gin either," Aladar countered. "I did a bit of research. What the Pocono restaurants lack in *savoir faire*, they make up with farm fresh produce, locally sourced meats and cheeses, imagination, and mountain ambiance."

"Sounds like they create their own expertise--one meaning of *savoir faire*. Let's check it out.*"

"I think we should try a place situated lakeside unimaginatively called, 'By the Water.' It's one of the closest to us in Jersey."

"Sounds wonderful. You know, Aladar, anything 'by the water' appeals to me—except maybe snakes!"

Our decision necessitated yet another drive to the mountains, albeit to a different area entirely.   This drive proved leisurely and without incident.

As we walked into "By the Water," I thought, *this restaurant could easily be found in the Alps.* There was wood everywhere. We were greeted by a smiling *maître d'hotel* who walked us intentionally, I'm certain, by a small man-made waterfall that flowed out of one wall over rocks strategically placed so that its bubbling water wove throughout the restaurant.

Local art hung on the opposite wall. A touch of the feeling of a German *biergarten* hit me. European atmosphere. I thought of Hemingway's line from *A Moveable Feast*, *"We're always lucky," … and like a fool I did not knock on wood. There was wood everywhere…."*

I succumbed to the urge to knock on wood there with Aladar. I didn't want us to make the same mistake Hemingway made. I wanted us to remain lucky. I lightly tapped a wall. The still smiling *maitre d'hotel* gave me a quizzical look as I tapped, but he didn't say anything. He seated us at a table next to huge windows that overlooked the lake—no wood nearby.

[183]

He's probably wondering why I tap tapped on the wall, but an explanation would take too long and be too much like a lecture not a conversation. I mean had he ever read A Moveable Feast? *Admittedly, it wasn't one of Hemingway's blockbusters.* With that thought, I turned my eyes and thoughts to the view and food.

From here the vista was truly breathtaking. Even the blue napkins on the table accentuated the blue of the lake. I thought of the Lochs in Scotland, of castles, of the fabulous wedding, of the family. I thought about Gladys and wondered how her honeymoon around the world was going.

Aladar interrupted my thinking by ordering the 'Smoked Gouda Fondue for Two' as an appetizer. I loved the place all the more when I discovered they carriedmy favorite Chalk Hill Chardonnay—the waiter assured me, "all the time."

"Then we must come back," I said. Aladar immediately ordered it to accompany our dinner.

As we ate, I asked, "Aladar, please tell me how that Glock, placed as it was almost next to Jane's breast, figures into this murder."

"What did Hitchcock call something like that in his movies? A MacGuffin? It's really nothing at all," Aladar said.

"But it was at the murder scene?" I protested.

"Exactly. You care about it. You're curious about it, so it advances the tension as it does in Hitchock's films, but as best we could determine through our investigation, it holds no significance in and of itself to this crime. Someone may have put it there to throw us off."

[184]

"Interesting. Then explain to me why in the world Angelique would invite this Jane person to the cabin in the first place? Is Jane a MacGuffin, too?"

"Decidedly not," came Aladar's adamant and quick response. Dipping his bread into the lushness of the fondue, he continued, "Angelique needed a ride up the mountains; she needed someone to help her pack and unpack, someone to be on hand to help her. Jane was handy. Remember, Angelique is 86 years old."

"She has no official caregiver?" I asked, puzzled.

"Doesn't ordinarily need one, I assume. In the City everyone takes a cab or rides the subway."

"With all her money, you would think she'd have at the very least a live-in caregiver."

"Perhaps she values her privacy more," Aladar suggested. "She's not incapacitated in any way that I could see."

"But someone for companionship. Or maybe for convenience," I persisted.

"Elizabeth, I think she has a woman like you have Perla who comes in daily or when needed. But whatever, Angelique's help is not in the purview of our investigation."

"True." I said, dabbing a bit of cheese off my lips.

"I could get that off," Aladar said with that wink.

"I think not. Not in this bustling restaurant. People will think us senile."

"We could pretend."

"Aladar, you are being silly."

It must have been the way I said the word *silly* because Aladar asked, "Are you about to launch into

[185]

word play, Elizabeth. Right here in broad daylight in a public place no less?"

"Oh, let's," I said with tease in my voice, feeling playful. "I'll begin by giving credit to a young historian by the name of Spencer McDaniel who wrote an article 'The Fascinating Evolution of the Word Silly.' He's my kind of scholar. While studying Ancient Greek and Latin, McDaniel dabbled in ancient religions, mythology, folklore, (and you'll love this, Aladar)" I said as an aside, "gender and sexuality."

"Let the games begin...."

"Silly is a silly word because it has illy in it. Therefore, it even sounds silly." I began.

"Nonsense, I happen to know that Illy is a brand of coffee."

"So coffee is silly?"

"No, illy is an art collection."

"You stray. Illy is not silly."

"You are being willy-nilly."

"*Au contraire.*" Then we both chuckled.

Chapter Forty-Eight

So, as it turns out, over pan-seared Chilean Bass in a cozy restaurant tucked into the foothills of Pennsylvania, I disclosed the murderer to Aladar.

"Fate? How did you ever arrive at that conclusion?" Aladar asked when I told him. He pushed his chair back and just stared at me, repeating, "Fate? I never would have thought it was Fate! I thought you had decided it was Jane or Mary."

"Woman's prerogative to change her mind," I said in my defense. "I'm not talking about intent here; I'm talking about what factually happened."

"Okay. I'm following you."

"I rethought my previous assumption and began considering Jane in earnest after our visit to Mr. Sneg's establishment. No" I corrected myself, "it began before that, way before that—perhaps with that word game you contrived about eyes, that word association game using the Eye of Horus that you initiated with Angelique and me."

"How so?"

"It was the phrase 'snake eyes' that struck me. A gambler's phrase. You know how I love words, silly me," I said with a tip of my wine glass and an exaggerated emphasis on the word *silly*.

"I do know that."

"The term 'snake eyes' refers to losers because if two thrown dice end up with one pip showing—one on each die—that is the lowest possible roll."

"I knew that."

[187]

"Me too. So, keeping 'loser' in my brain, I turned to the etymology of the word *snake.* There I found some interesting words, among them Mr. Sneg's name. It's an Indo-Europeanroot. Fits what he does almost too weirdly. But I also found the name *Schnake,* which happens to be Jane's last name."

"I knew that, too. Remember Sister Agnes? But I put no stock in it." Aladar admitted. "That's either too weird, coincidental, or one of those Aristotelian applications."

"True enough. But the bug bit. I had to dig deeper," I continued.

"Of course, you did, Elizabeth."

"Turns out that Schnake is a Norweigan name, probably originally German. The word itself, interestingly, comes closer to meaning *mosquito* than *snake,* but it can also apply to an annoying person. Other than that, I hit a dead end with *an annoying loser* the best connotation I could muster. Yet that phrase became annoying, like that mosquito. That annoying connection of snake to Jane took hold.

"So, I tried another approach—more direct, much more direct. I called Jane and asked her about her hobbies."

"You actually called another one of our suspects?"

"I did. At first, she was reluctant to talk to me knowing we are investigating things, but eventually because I kept bringing up snakes and she's obviously an ophidiophile...

"A what?"

"An ophidiophile—a lover of snakes. By the way,

the attraction in her case may even have become sexual over the years—but I'm no psychologist. I hit gold. She wanted to talk. I mean, that woman has a boa constrictor as a pet! Even calls him Boa—with a capital B. She admitted to me that even as a young girl she was fascinated with snakes."

"That was pretty gutsy of you to call her."

"Her admitting her fascination, led to my next question, "What fascinates you most about snakes, Jane?" I tried to sound calm.

"The many varieties of them," she said, "I think snakes have gotten a bad rap. Most people find them repulsive because of all the stories and myths. Even in the Harry Potter books, the boys who get in trouble the most are called the "Slytherins." Their colors are green and silver; their crest is a snake."

"Aladar, did you know that a group of snakes is called a 'slither'?"

"I did not."

"I didn't either. Fits the Potter books. But let me tell you the rest of my conversation with Jane. "

"I asked her, 'What variety of snake is your favorite or fascinates you most? The boa constrictor?' I offered. 'I mean since you have one as a pet?' I persisted, putting words in her mouth."

"Actually, no, if I could have any snake in the world, I'd want Australia's *Inland Taipan*. It's a rare and reclusive one but quite beautiful with its charcoal-colored head and that gold stripe down its body."

Aladar, that's when I noticed how her voice changed. She became excited, silly (in the erotic sense of that word) almost.

[189]

"Is it toxic?" I asked.

"Oh, yes. It's highly toxic plus it has an enzyme that accelerates its venom once in the victim's body," her voice growing even more animated.

"And that appeals to you?"

"What appeals to me is that intrinsic ability to debilitate its victim. Once that venom is in someone's body, it does all the work."

"The work?"

"The killing."

Chapter Forty-Nine

Aladar, Detective Whimsey tells me that in a far back room of Angelique's home they found a collection of what he called 'lady's pocketbooks.'

"Quaint."

"Yes, I haven't heard that term in years. Nevertheless, the information is worthy."

"In what way?"

"Apparently, several pieces are missing. Since no one has been there in weeks, the dust on the shelves is the dead give-a-way."

"That is significant because....?"

"Because the murderer is also a thief."

"And that's significant because...?

"Because of what was taken."

"Enlighten me."

"The two purses that were takenfrom the collection are snake related. The absence of dust in the shape of those purses gave us the clue, then Angelique confirmed that fact."

Chapter Fifty

"Well, Elizabeth, 'It's all over but the shouting!'"

"True enough, Aladar. This proved a most interesting case."

"What made the case for you, 'Grand Auntie, Sleuth Personified'?" Aladar said as he gave me one of his cuddly hugs.

Relaxing in his arms, I said, "There were a series of clues. Certainly, your work with the computer enhanced digitization of the bite provided scientific proof, but for me, the missing purses and the visit to Jane's apartment did it."

"Explain, please."

"It's where we found several pages of the same stationery that was used for that horrid note and the Eye of Horus drawing. That stationery in Jane's apartment provided the nail in the coffin and solidified the entire case."

"There goes Grand Auntie again!" With that, Aladar released me and walked over to the counter where he prepared some drinks and nibbles. He carried a tray of both to the table in front of the sofa and said, "Let's drink and nibble our celebration to another successfully solved case."

After a couple bites and a few sips, I said, "I'm always intrigued by the density of some people's beliefs."

"What do you mean?"

"Jane believing no one would suspect her. Her blatant admission to me over the phone about her love of snakes, I should say her sick love of snakes, was almost insulting."

"So that did the trick? Once you found out she loved snakes?"

"I don't think it was just one thing. I think it was a series of things, one clue fitting inside another like the pieces in a jig-saw puzzle. One piece fitting the other until the entire picture became clear. It began with the curious but unlikely love affair between Rosa Bloomfield and Kensington Astor eventually ending with the enigmatic Jane Schnake."

"Do you always think of our cases like jigsaw puzzles?"

"Not always, but this case came to me in pieces. When Detective Whimsey and I visited Jane's apartment, everything became crystal clear—all the pieces fell into place."

"You see the pieces and then you talk through them to their meanings?"

"Not immediately. But that's when I begin applying abductive reasoning. Whimsey and I saw the vivarium with the boa; then we saw another vivarium with a strange looking snake..."

"...I think all snakes are strange looking," Aladar chimed in.

"Me too, but this one was smaller but more vicious looking. It was a charcoal-chocolate brown with a beige belly. Funny vee-shaped designs ran along its form like a gold stripe. 'I don't like the look of that one,' Whimsey told me as he backed away from the enclosure. I didn't like its looks either."

"Again, Elizabeth, I don't like the look of most snakes."

"Later another detective told us that scary-looking snake was an Inland Taipan," I said.

"It's one of the most dangerous snakes in the world," the detective explained.

"And you saw it up close?" Aladar asked.

"I shudder when I think of it. I shudder thinking that we actually stood by its cage, that we were close enough to touch the snake—or scarier yet—the snake could have touched us, could have bitten us." *What in the world would a woman in an apartment want with two snakes*? I thought at the time."

"I see your abductive reasoning at work."

"Those clues coupled with all the previous information from Sister Agnes and then about childhood traumas, snake purses, thefts, school-girl jealousies, finally, the forensic psychologist suggesting Jane's depravity about snakes was enough for me to take another look."

"Take another look at what?"

"The body. When I did take another look, I found one almost infinitesimal puncture mark on Jane! The forensic specialists verified my find."

"So you reasoned that this extremely poisonous Inland Taipan didn't bite Angelique?"

"I did, plus the lab insisted the puncture mark was not a bite. Yet its venom killed her nonetheless."

"How did that happen?"

"By Fate—just as I told you."

"Jane intended to inject the venom she had milked from that Inland Taipan into Angelique, but she didn't get the chance. Her plan never came to fruition."

"Why not?"

"Because Fate intervened." Just as Jane was about to clobber or engage Angelique in a fight—she intended a real cat fight, I'm sure. One that would cover up everything. Ever see one on TV or in the movies?"

"Not that I recall." I could tell Aladar was eager for me to cut to the chase.

"There was that famous one at the pond on *Dynasty—purse hitting, name calling, scratching, punching*—women can become fierce. They disregard rules. Anyway, I stray. Just as Jane was about to execute her well-thought-out plan, Mary entered the house."

"Mary? How did she do that?" Aladar asked.

"She had a key. Angelique had given her a key when she first purchased the cabin. 'Mary, I want you to keep this key someplace safe—just in case.' You know, Aladar, that notion most people hold that it's a good idea for someone else, someone neutral, to have a key to your premises in case something happens."

Aladar nodded. "We did that with Pheme and Russ."

"Exactly.When Angelique went missing the second time, Mary thought she better check the cabin—a likely place since that's where Angelique escaped to the first time she went missing. As she drove up, she spotted Jane's car, did some sound reasoning on her own, figuring it wasn't anyone's car she knew. She used the key Angelique had given her and entered the cabin."

[195]

"That's when all hell broke loose?"

"Can you imagine it, Aladar? Imagine the moment when Jane saw Mary. All her conniving and planning were about to go up in smoke! So, Jane attacked Mary!"

"Now that must have been a cat fight," Aladar said.

"Indeed! At first, caught by surprise as she was, Mary went on the defensive, but she soon gathered her wits. Being bigger and stronger, she overwhelmed Jane, but in that crucial struggle the syringe Jane had prepared so carefully for Angelique punctured her own arm, ironically just about where the Eye of Horus tattoo was on Angelique's arm—the soft, fleshy part. It immediately went to work. Jane was dead within minutes.

So, we could say the famous Eye of Horus *did* protect Angelique after all.

"The first bite was my first solid clue—the bite Jane gave Angelique when she ransacked her apartment. The bite made out of jealousy. Then your electron microscope imagining of teeth marks proved it to be Jane and that science coupled with my abductive reasoning solidified everything. Aladar, I reasoned, whoever bit her ultimately killed her. And I was 100% correct although technically and ultimately Fate was the murderer, claiming the rightful victim."

"Philosophy and science—an unbeatable combination."

"In this case, that combination proved to be fatal for Jane."

# Chapter Fifty-One

"Oh, Aladar, it feels so good to be home and have a normal pet like Coco, jumping her greeting instead of a snake slithering!"

"I agree."

"Sometimes I think we are too normal."

"I think we're just fine, Elizabeth."

"I found several messages on my phone."

"That's pretty normal. From whom?"

"Pheme, Glady, Ande, Umbuya, Cathy, the House of Chanel, and Franny.

"That's quite a list. And?" Aladar asked.

"Pheme invited us over with her usual urgency: 'Come over ASAP. I have big news and then bigger news that I must share in person!' She is the mama of hyperbole, I swear!"

"With our dear, dear Pheme that news can be anything from the twins spitting up again, to a cute outfit, to finding a dead body," Aladar quipped.

"Aladar, I fear you are getting to know my family far too well! Listen to this one that Glady texted from India: 'Dr. Henson and I will be home well before Christmas. We're also bringing an elephant—maybe two. Plan accordingly.'"

"After snakes, an elephant or two would be welcome!" he said. We laughed. "But how in the world does Gladys think we could possibly plan for that contingency?"

[197]

"Only Glady knows. Sometimes her humor is so sideways."

"Knowing Gladys, I wouldn't be a bit surprised if she isn't already arranging a party in the elephant's honor!" Aladar said giving me an affection squeeze."

"Really, Aladar, Glady isn't that eccentric," thinking to myself *she could very well ship an elephant or two here; and, if she did, she could very well have a party to honor them. Any excuse for a party—that's my sister!*

"Don't count on this just being a joke. She's got the money, the connections, the space, the time, and now the title—and an abiding love of animals. I wouldn't put anything past her. Probably turn that single elephant or two into some sort of investment. Make another million while she's at it!" We both chuckled. Knowing Gladys, we couldn't discount anything!

"Any other messages?"

"Oh, yes. Ande texted this: 'Text me when you get back. I have an idea.'"

"Second only to Grammy Gladys' ideas, Ande's scare me," Aladar said.

"Well, then gird your loins. I'll be following up with a text to Ande this afternoon. But Aladar, I'm pleased to hear this one from Sea. Seems like he's finally getting his bearings after Trés' murder."

"What did he say?"

He and Loraine want to host Christmas dinner this year for the family. He asks us not to make other plans.

"That's fabulous, Elizabeth, just fabulous. Good for him! I assume we shall be going?"

"Of course! But here's a surprise—one from Umbuya: 'Call me when you return.'"

"Isn't she your former classmate from college, the one from Africa, the one who gave that powerful interview?"

"Yes, which reminds me. We have that reunion coming up like soon—very soon. We better give that some thought. And speaking of classmates, Cathy left a message. I re-played it so Aladar could hear it: 'Call me. It's about Hanaka. All good.'

I certainly hope the good news is about Hanaka's eyes."

"Is that it?"

"No. The House of Chanel, listen: 'Gown is ready. Requested reconstruction has been made. Text us.'

"That means I'll have that lovely gown for the reunion. I'm so happy. It's such a waste to wear a bridesmaid's gown only once. With its classic design and the redesign I requested, I should get several events out of it."

"Since when did you become so frugal?" Aladar teased.

"Since meeting or re-meeting a struggling forensic scientist."

"I'm hardly struggling—NOW—but there was a time." Aladar gently pushed me onto the sofa and began hisgrowling.

"No," I protested. "Not yet. There is one more message."

[199]

"Well, okay, check it out but then we must celebrate our homecoming," Aladar said chucking me under my chin and brushing his lips along mine just enough to send me those tingles and shivers."

With tingles still going down my spine, I turned on the messages again: "Franny here: Do you have plans for Christmas?"

# Chapter Fifty-Two

Time to answer all the messages, I thought. *Ande's idea is a good one. With Grammy Gladys back home, she wants the family to conjure some sort of surprise party.*

When I texted Ande, she texted back,

Much as Grammy loves parties, Lizbet, I don't ever remember anyone giving her one as a surprise. We gave her parties—you know, birthday, anniversaries, for her successes with PARA, but never one as a surprise.

I texted back to Ande: I like your idea. Let's meet for lunch in the next week or so and plan something. In the meantime, I'll be thinking, and you do the same. By the way, Ande, Grammy hinted at bringing an elephant from India—maybe two. Perhaps we should factor that into our plans.

Almost immediately Ande responded: OMG! Really? I wouldn't put anything past her.

Then I turned my attention to Umbuya. I called her, "Hi Umbuya, I'm back.

"Hi Elizabeth. Good to hear from you."

"You asked me to call?"

"Yes, I want to talk to you about an idea I have. It concerns Angelique and you."

"I'm interested."

"Let's us five underwrite a 'chair' at our alma mater. We could each pitch in a modest amount to kick it off, have a lawyer draw up the stipulations, etc.—you know all that legal business that goes into such things, and have a remembrance in perpetuity of our detective

workon behalf of Angelique. We could give the
scholarship a name and announce it at the reunion.
What do you think?"

"That's a lovely idea, Umbuya. Leave it to you to
think of something so giving. Call the Girls. We can
meet sometime soon before the reunion to hammer
out the detailsso we'll have everything in order for the
announcement at the reunion."

"Will do."

I couldn't wait to hear what Cathy had to say
about Hanaka.

"Hi Cathy, you have good news for me?"

"How was Scotland? You must regale me with all
the details soon."

"I will. Actually, Umbuya has an idea and wants
us to consider it, so she'll be contacting you soon so we
can all meet. I can bore all of you at the same time
about Scotland."

"You never bore, Elizabeth. You tell a story
better than anyone. But let me tell you the good news.
Hanaka went to an eye specialist of in Switzerland while
you were in Scotland—one who has a very impressive
title and a string of degrees after his name. This doctor
examined her eyes over several days, using the newest,
top-of-the-line equipment and held out quite a
promise. He actually thinks he can reverse this
deterioration process that would blind her."

"That's a miracle!" I said.

"She's over the moon happy about it. We need
to celebrate her."

"Let's do something special for her at the
reunion."

[202]

"Good idea."

"Hi Franny, Elizabeth here. You wanted to talk about Christmas?"

"Yes, I have no plans and hate being alone on that day of all days. You know I'm not clever enough to wheedle an invitation, so I'm asking outright if I could do something with you on that day."

"No need to wheedle, Franny, I'm quite certain the family will be having dinner at Sea's—you are more than welcome to join us. I'll keep you posted on the details."

"Thanks, Elizabeth, you're a true friend. I can't wait to see you and hear all about Scotland."

I saved my dear Pheme for last.

"Hi Pheme!"

"Lisbet! I can't wait to tell you the news!"

"What news, Pheme? Your message made it sound as if there were two pieces of news. Was I wrong?"

"No, not at all! First, Dr. Ali confirmed that Russ and I are having another set of twins!"

"How wonderful, Pheme. Now you are doubly doubly or is it quadruply blessed as is the family? Imagine four little ones, and you thinking you could never conceive!"

"This time she's certain it's a boy and a girl—fraternal!"

"Even better, Pheme. Are you already thinking of outfits? For sure, you don't want them dressed alike!"

"Of course! And Grand Auntie, we're going to name them after our great grandparents—Adam and

[203]

Zebeta. We'll probably anglicize the pronunciation of Zebeta to Zee-beta, rather than the Scz-beta sound that is so pretty in Polish but so hard for us to say. We think, we'll call them 'A' and 'Z' for short!"

"Leave it to you, Pheme, to think of everything. I love it! I love that you are honoring Adam and Zebeta, and I love the nicknames. I love this second set of twins already."

"I hoped you would approve, Lizbeth. I'm so happy you have approved. You and Ande are such sticklers about names and words. She liked my idea, too."

"Good. What was the other piece of news?"

"I hope you're as positive about it as you are about the twins.'"

"I'm sure I'll be."

"Grammy Gladys is giving Russ and me—giving to us outright, no strings attached—the property next to yours!"

"Why! That's grand news!"

"She was worried you'd think it unfair to the others, but Ande isn't interested in ever leaving New York City, and Loraine and Sea are content with where they are and with what they have. Both couples are set financially."

"I have no problem with it, Pheme, after all, we all know that property will stay in the family—especially with these four new additions!"

"Grammy said, with four little ones, it would be—how did she say it—'prudent and commonsensical' to have you—meaning me—close to Grand Auntie—for her sake and yours."

[204]

"She's right. She's always right. But not only
that, it will be my joy and Aladar's to have so many little
ones around. They keep you young, you know. Even
the brain research confirms that. God bless, Grammy
Gladys

"What's this?" I asked, as Aladar laid at dinner a beautifully wrapped box about 8" X 4" in front of me next to a glass of my favorite wine.

"It's called a present, a gift, largesse, freebee, offering, windfall, contribution, bestowal, boon," he said as if he had memorized a list.

"You forgot my favorite word in that category."

"What's that?"

"Lagniappe, as in a bonus. I am quite sure whatever is in this box is a bonus."

"Why do you think that, My Dear?"

"Lagniappe's main connotation is 'really not deserved.'"

"Ah! But you do deserve this. Besides, it's symbolic and you always love something symbolic. This is one rewardsyou; this is decidedly one you are most deserving of receiving," Aladar said.

"Why?"

"You solved another case."

"So, this is the icing on the cake?"

"Think of it more as a fringe benefit!"

"But you solved it, too, and I got you nothing."

"Then think of this as a tribute to your incredible abductive reasoning—this gift will always remind you of this case."

"I can't wait to open it. Drum roll, please."

With that, Aladar began to hit the table with his fingers, at first lightly and then progressively with more force. It was so dramatic, it made me laugh. He laughed, too.

I untied the ribbon with a simple pull of it and then tore off the paper. What I found was a professionally marbleized box that resembled a book, a book with a label inlaid into its cover. In gold letters it read:

Montblanc Meisterstück
Agatha Christie
LIMITED EDITION

The black 'book' spine contained the same information.

"This is darling," I said, already loving the book idea, appreciating the presentation, but still not knowing exactly what was inside, although 'Montblanc' should have been a big clue, although I was too excited to reason it all out.

"Go ahead and open it," Aladar urged. My mind momentarily raced back to that night at his home when he gifted me with a beautiful Hanro nightgown. He had such a pleased look on his face. Then it raced farther back to Christmas, to his gift from Tiffany's—same look. I saw that identical look now. Whatever was in that box, Aladar was pleased with himself for getting it.

Once I opened it, I found the lid lined in black velvet, the base of the box lined in black satin. The box itself promised elegance and elegance is what I received. Nestled in that satin and velvet was a Montblanc ink pen, signed by Agatha Christie. "Oh, Aladar," I breathed. "It's beautiful and so different."

"Look closely," he prompted. "Why it has a sterling silver snake on it! And the snake has two ruby

[207]

eyes!" I exclaimed in awe. Wrapped around the cap of the pen were two strands of sterling silver that literally slithered down the cap forming a snake. Two perfectly cut rubies were its eyes. The way the jeweler cut the silver approximated its scales. I held in my hands a work of art.

I was aware Aladar was talking, "Dear One, I know this isn't as expensive a pen as an Aurora Diamante, but it holds levels of significance. By the way, I also bought you a bottle of that ink Faber Castell— now nothing you write can be erased!"

"Oh, I realize the significance of this gift, Aladar, and you know me and symbolism. Second only to words, I value the symbology of things."

"I was counting on that. Agatha Christie has nothing on you, Elizabeth. And you not only write about crimes, you actually solve them. This last one was a doozie with those snakes and that snake-crazed Jane involved. You most certainly not only deserve this gift, but you earned it. I love you so much, Elizabeth Armory," Aladar said as he smiled at me, taking me in his arms.

"I do love you, Aladar Gallant," I said reaching up and running my hands through his hair. Just at that moment, a thought popped into my head. *In a film noir, there would be a slow fadeout as Nick takes Nora in his arms. Here on the reality of Earth One, things aren't really that different.*

Aladar reached for me, slowly bringing me closer to him, tenderly kissing me, and then gently leading me upstairs. "I'd carry you, Elizabeth, but after I carried you

[208]

those few steps into that cabin in the Poconos, I realized all future 'carrying' will have to be symbolic."

"Not to worry, dear Aladar," I said smiling, "you already know how much I love a good symbol and your kisses are symbols enough—the best kind.

Chapter Fifty-Four

My Beloved Du,

Here I am back home. I've only been gone a little over a month, but it seems like years so much has happened. Gladys and Dr. Henson are on their way back from a honeymoon around the world—maybe with elephants—after a wedding and reception that befits the royalty they are.

Russ and Pheme are going to have twins again—a boy and girl this time, which they will name Adam and Zebeta—A and Z. They are overjoyed as are we all.

Gladys flat out gave them all that property next to ours. We'll have a virtual compound, and I couldn't be happier about it.

Sea seems to be coming out of his depression. Sea and Loraine are going to host Christmas dinner this year. Ande continues to be her creative self, and as Gladys said what seems like years ago, "The cubs are getting this thing called life right."

I miss you. I will always miss you: I will always love you, but you do need to know that Aladar has proclaimed his love to me and I to him. I brooded about it; somehow it seems so different, not right on the one hand since you were and always will be the love of my life, but so right on the other hand somehow, too, because Aladar is so perfect for me at this time of my life. As Mama Zebeta always said, "Nie mozesz zyc ze zmartymi, you can't live with the dead." I am hoping in whatever dimension you now are, my dearest Du, you understand that.

As you probably already suspect, this will be my last letter until I see you in that other dimension.

Chapter Fifty-Five

Our sixty-fifth university reunion was what we used to call "a bash!" Heaven only knows what young people call it today! Held at our old college haunt, the Waldorf Astoria, that icon of luxury and wealth during the early and into the middle 20th Century, it begged reminiscences. In its day, the Waldorf depicted the best of the *Arte Deco* period, but since it has been recently remodeled, it reimagines the future.

The six of us planned to share a table in their famous Grand Ballroom, the very same ballroom where we, as sophomores in college, held our prom. This Grand Ballroom has been protected by the New York City Landmark's Preservation Commission, so to me it still feels like 1957.

Since none of us have living spouses sitting here with us, we resemble an older rendition of *Sex and the City*. In the background a live orchestra plays a vintage Guy Lombardo favorite. I fully expect Eddy Duchin's sweet music any minute as encore. After all he met his socialite wife Marjorie Oelrichs at the Waldorf.

I loved how Chanel redesigned my bridesmaid's gown—taking that rather dated scoop neckline and remaking the gown strapless and sexy and modern. They fooled with the hemline, too, keeping it in vogue.

The others looked smashing, too. Hanaka decided to wear that family crested kimono with a newly designed Obi she sent for directly from Japan. Cathy found something quite suitable in a vintage shop in the Hamptons. Our dear Franny wore dowdy brown, but we loved her all the more for it.

But Umbuya, Umbuya OMG! she entered the ballroom with panache, wearing a vibrant metallic and silk floor-length gown with wide sleeves and matching head piece.

"We call our national dress *kpokpo*, but this is our traditional gown for special events, simply called the 'print.'"

We gushed like college girls over its gold threading and black print open-stitch design. Umbuya wore it over a pair of tie-up trousers. Its cobalt blue sleeves matched its head tie, which made her look seven feet tall.

If Hanaka was our Japanese Princess, surely Umbuya was our African Queen.

"I'm missing Angelique," Cathy said. She always seemed to give words to what everyone else thought. Looking around, she continued, "She's late. Where can she be? That worries me. We can't have her missing again—not tonight of all nights!"

I worried, too. We raised our glasses to Angelique. "Hear! Hear! To our Angelique!" And as if we were making a movie, Angelique appeared at the entrance to the ballroom.

"Who is that woman with her?" Cathy whispered, squinting her eyes. "I don't recognize her from our class?" None of us had any idea. I motioned to our waiter indicating we needed two places added to our table. In the true style of a top-drawer establishment, chairs appeared magically, and place settings appeared in a matter of minutes. Before

[212]

Angelique and her guest wove their way to the table, all was in readiness.

Clad in a bodycon sheath dress of silver that hugged her figure so clingy I fear what might happen when she sat down, Angelique carried the Isabelle Fayette minaudiére called 'The Flower Pot.'

"I just had to show you my latest acquisition," she said simultaneously placing it on the table for us to see and slipping into one of the two waiting seats while ordering a Cosmo. She motioned to the woman to take the other seat; she ordered a Cosmo for her, too. "I bought it to celebrate the solution to this case that Elizabeth and her forensic fellow have been chasing. Somehow flowers, in any form, seemed in order. But first, I want you Girls to meet my sister, my long-lost sister, Mary Astor."

I restrained a gasp. Could this stylish, attractive woman be the frumpy cleaning woman from the high rise?

"I want to hear the whole story," Franny, who was always a bit out of it, begged, sipping her drink. I made a mental note to have Sea be sure to have her favorite brand of vodka, plus plenty of cranberry juice, lime juice, and triple sec on hand when she came for dinner at Christmas.

"Now is as good a time as any," Hanaka agreed. "You start, Elizabeth. I understand it was you who figured it all out."

"I'll make it brief, Girls. It all started when Angelique called me about an ominous note she received."

"What did it say?" Cathy asked.

[213]

"Life isn't fair. I'm going to kill you."

"That *is* ominous," they chorused accentuating *is*.

"My forensic friend, Aladar Gallant, got his team together to study the note."

"Come on now, Elizabeth, I hear this Aladar fellow is becoming more than a friend lately," Cathy said.

"That's another story," I protested, but I could feel my face reddening. The Girls giggled. *Are we back in college?* I asked myself, grinning.

"All this happened as we were about to step on the plane headed for Scotland and my sister Gladys' wedding, so I promised Angelique that Dr. Gallant and I would look into everything when we returned. I warned her to be careful."

"But she wasn't careful, was she?" Cathy interjected, looking directly at Angelique who took her cue and looked demurely away.

"Well, she received another note, but we didn't know about this one until we returned. This second one, in my opinion, was even more ominous with no words just a drawing of what Angelique identified as the 'Eye of Horus' staring at us off the paper. In the meantime, one of her most valuable *minaudières* went missing.

"The Swarovski pistol?" Hanaka asked.

"No, apparently one even more valuable. Anyway, now there were many threads sticking out all over just begging to be pulled."

"Then the plot thickened. Angelique went missing for several weeks. I located her, but she was so

[214]

frightened, she literally hid herself in her own home in the Pocono Mountains. Dr. Gallant and I went into detective mode, and as you know, all of us were all suspects for a time, given we were among the last to see her."

"Then I heard on TV she was found dead," Cathy contributed to the story. "I called Elizabeth."

"We were no longer concerned about an heiress from the gossip columns missing but about a dear friend who was slain," Franny summarized.

"Well, she wasn't—slain, that is. I disregarded all of us as suspects, narrowing the suspect list to the doorman, Angelique's sister..."

"Who I didn't know as my sister," Angelique interjected, "Didn't even know I had a sister..." looking and smiling at Mary and patting her hand. Mary just smiled back at her.

"...and a woman, named Jane, who picked up soils at Angelique's high rise. After interrogations, I dismissed the doorman. That left this extremely jealous sister who had been disowned by their quite wealthy father and timid mother, and this Jane person, who seemed almost invisible. She, too, harbored jealousy towards Angelique since before high school."

Mary sat still as stone through this. I wondered what she was thinking.

Continuing with Mary in mind, sitting like she was, right there among us, I tried to be tactful. "After interviewing them both, visiting their living areas, and employing my abductive reasoning techniques, I was certain it was Jane. We also had what's called in the field 'hard evidence,' proving I was correct."

[215]

"Is it true, Elizabeth, you're called 'The Grand Auntie of Sleuthdom?'" Franny asked, awe in her voice.

"Pish. Posh." I said, "My family calls me Grand Auntie because of my age. When I began sleuthing with Dr. Aladar Gallant, someone added 'of Sleuthdom.' I rather like it."

"So do we," they said in unison, all smiles.

"How many cases have you solved," Cathy asked. She never knew any bounds—if the thought entered her head, it came out her mouth, but that was our Cathy.

"Let's see..." I paused to think. "There was Trés' murder that started it all. Then I got involved with the Mafia...."

Franny gasped. "You did?"

"Not in the way you think, Franny. But do you all remember Giovanna Castalanno from college? We called her Vanna." They all nodded. "Well, she, in a round-a-bout way, drew me into the second case. After that, Aladar and I became a team—sort of the Nick and Nora, do you remember them from *The Thin Man* fame?" Again, they nodded. "Then along came Reggie and Bert, case number three. And now our dear Angelique numbers four."

"How exciting, Franny sighed. "My life now is just the same-old, same-old."

"Franny," I said, "I promise I will get you involved in my next case! Pinky promise." And then, as if we were in fourth grade, we locked pinky fingers.

"But I warn you, it might be dangerous."

"At eighty-six, I need some danger!"

[216]

We all just gaped at Franny. "Franny, you were always so cautious, so afraid of trying anything new—even a new hat—what's come over you?" I asked.

"Age, I guess. I want to make a difference—even if it's a little one before I go."

"I'll work on that with you, Franny. I promise."

Little did I know that a small clay figurine of a Pueblo 'storyteller doll' would help solve my next murder case. And little did I know that dear Franny would be more involved in solving that case than either she or I could even imagine right now.

"Speaking of promises," Angelique said, "I have spoken to my attorney. I have established a scholarship for young ladies of somewhat limited means who want to pursue their careers in the Humanities. The Scholarship will be named after my sister, The Mary Astor Humanities Scholarship." Angelique, ever the giver, then patted Mary's hand again.

"All of which reminds me," spoke up Umbuya. "I think we need to endow a chair in Elizabeth's name—something to do with sleuthing."

"Hear! Hear! The Girls chorused.

With that our waiter returned with another round of drinks. "I understand a celebration is in order," he began. He gestured to a man standing in the wings who came forward. Handsome in that Latino way, and barrel-chested in that way of male opera singers, Santiago de la Cada, presently the hottest tenor at the Met, stepped out from behind the curtains.

Good on her intention to do something for Hanaka, Angelique who had contacts everywhere, had gotten in touch with the Metropolitan Opera House to secure a tenor for our reunion.

Without introduction, and because he needed none, he said, "This aria is for Hanaka Haraka from 'The Girls'. He sang 'Nessun Dorna" ("No One Sleeps") from *Turando*. When he finished, we arose as one, along witheveryother person in the Ballroom and within earshot. We gave him a standing ovation and shots of 'Bravo!' We were all in tears, hugging each other, happy to be alive and together—happy for Hanaka's eyes, Cathy's inquisitiveness, Umbuya's grace, Franny's loyalty, Angelique's presence, and happy for her sister.

And me? I was just happy knowing Aladar waited for me.

**CODA**

"It's so good to have you back, Glady, but whatever made you have two, two elephantsfrom India shipped back?" I asked my sister as we at under our arbor and sipped Bridget's heavenly coffee brew, and as we gathered our Afghan blankets around ourselves against the cold, that early cold we cherished as it brought with it the promise of all good things winter. "One would have raised enough eyebrows."

"I have plans," Gladys confidently confided with a furtive smile.

"I bet you do; you always have plans."

"I think having plans gives me purpose, keeps me young—as does JUNGYU, and my beloved Doctor Henson, and you my dear sister, and...."

She trailed off as Bridget refilled our cups. They did, in fact, overflow. For that we were and remained grateful.

"Speaking of JUNGYU, did I tell you about Angelique's sister Mary?" I asked. "She had pock marks all over her face, Angelique insisted she try JUNGYU and already there is a visible difference. Those pock marks are fading."

"None of us at the reunion even recognized her. With the benefit of JUNGYU and makeup and dim lights, we couldn't even see those marks. Angelique took Mary to her hairstylist, too. Magic. Alferina lightened Mary's dingy hair and gave her low lights. That inspired Mary to go on a diet. Of course, Angelique, being so generous and so happy to have a sister, took her to Bruno, her

[219]

personal shopper at Bergdorf's, for a wardrobe. You can't believe how beautiful she looks."

"I can believe it, Lisbet."

"But the most astonishing transformation is with that arm of hers. Angelique found a doctor who specializes in Erb's Palsy. This doctor took Mary on as a unique case, given her age. He explained how her upper nerves and loss of muscle function in her arm and shoulder were the psroblem. He suggested corrective surgery, followed by a regime of exercises. She agreed. It seems to be working. Mary is regaining more and more use of her arm."

"Good for her!"

"But, Glady, back to you—TWO ELEPHANTS?" I was sure Glady could hear the protest in my tone.

"Sip your coffee, Lisbet, and I will share my plans. But first you must tell me how things are progressing with your forensic fellow. He made quite an impression at our wedding."

"What sort of impression?"

"Everyone remarked on how solicitous he was of you, how he must love you. Why, Lisbet, are you blushing? At your age?"